Gabbi's Goalie

A Curvy Girl Hockey Romance

Nichole Rose

CONTENTS

About the Book   1

Chapter One   3

Chapter Two   11

Chapter Three   18

Chapter Four   32

Chapter Five   48

Chapter Six   62

Chapter Seven   68

Chapter Eight   85

Chapter Nine   97

Chapter Ten   114

Chapter Eleven   124

Chapter Twelve   127

Chapter Thirteen   131

Chapter Fourteen   140

Epilogue   145

Author's Note   151

Silver Spoon After Dark   152

Truly Mine   154

Follow Nichole   157

Instalove Book Club   159

Nichole's Book Beauties   160

Also by Nichole Rose   161

About Nichole Rose   167

ABOUT THE BOOK

This over-the-top goalie refuses to crash and burn when it comes to the woman of his dreams.

Atlas Jacks

The moment I set eyes on Gabbi Sterling, I know she's mine.

Unfortunately, she doesn't agree.

Her brother owns my team.

Her best friend told a little white lie.

And my girl is giving me nine kinds of hell.

Right up until we get lost in the woods together.

Now, it's up to me to get her out safely.

There's just one problem.

I have a concussion and no clue where we are.

Gabbi Sterling

Atlas Jacks makes my blood boil...in more ways than one.

The oversized goalie is infuriating. He's also infuriatingly hot.

I thought he slept with my best friend, but I was wrong.

Now, I have no excuse for keeping him at a distance.

Except for the fact that my brother will kill us both.

I didn't mean to get us lost in the woods.

Or to end up in his arms.

But now that we're here, I'm not so sure I want us to be found.

Right up until his life depends on it, anyway.

I'll do whatever it takes to save the man I love.

CHAPTER ONE

Atlas

"Holy shit." I fumble my stick, staring at the curvy blonde who just stepped into the player box with Jordan Sterling, owner of the Silver Spoon Falls Falcons. She's bundled up as if she's visiting the Arctic Circle, the faux fur from her parka framing her heart-shaped face. Her doe eyes dart everywhere as she takes in the action on the ice, watching with avid interest.

"Holy shit, what?" Noah Diamante cranes his neck, trying to see what I'm staring at.

"Don't look at her," I growl, stepping in front of him to block his view. She's mine. I saw her first.

It's a ridiculous, juvenile thought...and yet it screams loudly anyway.

She's mine. At least, she will be as soon as I can make it happen.

"What the fuck? I was just trying to figure out why you suddenly look all fucking weird," Noah mutters.

"I don't look weird."

Shit. Do I look weird?

I'm dressed in my practice gear...which basically means I look like the Michelin Man. Fuck my life. She looks like a little winter fairy. I look like the damn Michelin Man. Being a goalie is killing my vibe.

Oh, well. At least I'm a goddamn artist in a net.

"You look like you're constipated."

I turn a dirty scowl on Noah. "Why are we even friends?"

"Beats me. But if you want to know who she is, you'd better be nice to me." He smirks, his dark eyes alight with humor.

"You know her?"

"I know her name."

I wait for him to tell me, but when he doesn't cough up the intel, I growl, "What is it?"

"Gabbi Sterling."

My future wife's name is Gabbi Sterling.

"Wait a damn minute." My stomach sinks. "Sterling? As in—"

"Yep. She's Jordan Sterling's little sister." Noah smacks me on the back, laughing as he skates away. "Good luck with that, big guy."

Fucking hell. My future wife is related to the billionaire who owns the Falcons, more or less making him my boss.

I watch her for a long moment, trying to figure out how the hell I'm going to convince Jordan to let me run away with his sister. He strikes me as the overprotective type. Actually, scratch that. He doesn't strike me that way. He *is* that way, point blank, period. I saw him in action when some drunk asshole tried to get handsy with our physical therapist.

Let's just say the guy is no longer a fan of the home team or Jordan Sterling.

Gabbi glances in my direction and our eyes meet. Hers are endless pools of melted chocolate. A lightning bolt hits me right in the chest, sending electric shocks throughout my system. Her eyes widen as if she feels the same intense spark.

My body lights up like a livewire, my cup getting painfully tight as my dick hardens. A grin stretches across my face, unbidden. How can I not smile? I'm staring at my future and it's bright as hell.

She is not on the same page. She looks like she's staring at someone who makes her blood boil. And not in a good, sexy way. Her lips compress into a line as her little chin comes up. Pure ire filters through her expression, as if just the sight of me pisses her off.

What the fuck? What did I do?

I've only known she existed for two minutes. That's not nearly enough time for her to decide she hates me. She hasn't even officially met me yet. And not to brag or anything, but I'm fucking awesome.

I launch myself across the ice to work on proving it to her, all my attention focused on my end goal. I've never had an actual marriage fantasy in my life, but I'm hearing wedding bells.

Four of my teammates have gotten married in the last few months. Coach did too. A motherfucker is lonely and not afraid to admit it. Unlike a lot of guys in the league, I'm not interested in one-night stands or sowing wild oats or any of that shit. I want the same forever my parents found together when they were freshmen in college. I've just never found anyone who interested me enough to pursue it.

Looks like I just found out why.

"Jacks!" Miles Tempest shouts, his voice full of warning. "Look ou–"

Something cracks me in the back of the head hard enough to rattle my skull. Pain rips through my head, bringing tears to my eyes. I trip over my skates and fall hard.

I land on my back, staring up at the rafters far overheard.

Either I'm seeing shit, or there's actually a bird up there, flying around.

"Fuck!" Reid Lawless shouts. "Someone get Doc Jessup!"

"Atlas!" Noah skids to a stop, throwing up ice from his skates. He drops to his knees beside me, his worried face looming into focus above mine. "Talk to me, man."

I blink up at him, trying to think through the pounding headache. Jesus Christ. For a bookworm, Miles is a menace with a stick. That hurt like a son of a bitch.

"Say something, Atlas," Noah growls. "Talk to me."

"I'm getting married. And there's a bird in the rafters."

His shoulders slump, relief and amusement washing through his expression. Before he can say anything, Coach Marrow, Miles, and Colter Bayliss skate up.

"Goddammit, Jacks," Coach kneels on the ice near my head. "If we have to bench you, you're going to wish you took more than a puck to the head. Where the fuck is your helmet?"

"He got distracted," Noah answers for me.

"By what this time?" Coach asks as if I'm a toddler who can't stay on task. Which is honestly fair. I spend half my time in a net, talking to my damn self. I get bored. Sue me. "We haven't even been on the ice five minutes."

"Can I help?" a dulcet voice asks. "I'm a nurse. Well, nearly."

"He got distracted by her," Noah mutters quietly.

"Nearly a nurse?" Colter nudges Miles. "That sounds ominous."

I ignore them, rolling my head to the side, seeking her out. She's a few paces behind Noah, her hood pulled back.

Her short golden-brown hair is wild around her face, little pieces dancing from static. Without the hood, she's even more gorgeous, glowing from the inside out.

Little lines of worry furrow her brows. How the fuck can someone be adorable and sexy at the same time?

"Yes. Help," I rasp. "It hurts."

She steps forward instantly. Noah shifts over, giving her room to squeeze in. "Where is the pain worst?" she asks, dropping to her knees beside me.

"My balls."

"Jesus Christ," Colter mutters, choking on a laugh.

"Jacks!" Coach Marrow shoots me a death glare. At least, I assume he's shooting me a death glare. I don't look at him to confirm, but I feel his disapproving glower. For a man who just got married, he's awful cranky.

"Um, I think he has a concussion," Gabbi says, her cheeks turning pink. She holds up three fingers. "How many fingers?"

"One without a ring."

"What day is it?"

"The first day of the rest of my life."

Coach Marrow mutters a curse.

"Who is the president?"

"An asshole."

Gabbi's expression is rife with worry.

"Don't fret, fairy. My brain is fine," I murmur, trying to soothe her. "I got all your questions right."

"You didn't get any of them right, Atlas," Colter says.

"What? Yes, I did."

Her finger doesn't have a ring on it, Bruce Gorden—the league president—is an asshole, and today is the first day of the rest of my life.

Gabbi reaches toward me and then hesitates. "I'm going to check your head, Atlas."

"You know my name."

"Yes." She prods at the back of my head, probing at the knot already forming there. It hurts like a motherfucker.

"How?" I growl. "Son of a bitch, that hurts."

"You need a CT Scan."

"How?"

"At the hospital."

"How do you know my name, baby?"

Her eyes flash as they lock on mine, a little of that same fire from earlier peeping out. "Hollie," she snaps before looking away from me to Coach. "He needs a CT. He may have a concussion."

I don't. I've had more than my fair share over the years. It comes with the territory when you tend goal. This feels nothing like those.

I'm more concerned with why my future wife is pissed that I know our physical therapist. I've barely even spoken to her.

But I don't get the opportunity to ask. Doc Jessup comes running in, and Gabbi quickly steps aside.

My last glimpse of her is of her round ass as she walks away.

Newsflash: it does absolutely nothing to help the pain in my balls.

CHAPTER TWO

Atlas

"Jesus. It's crowded in here tonight."

"*You*," Colter says, pointing at me, "shouldn't even be here. You have a concussion."

"My brain is fine," I lie. Despite all my claims to the contrary, my brain is not actually fine. I spent half of yesterday undergoing a battery of tests, all of which confirmed Gabbi's suspicions. I have a concussion. It's my second one in less than a year, so they're taking the shit seriously.

I'm riding the bench for the next two weeks. Another concussion and I'm out for the season. It's not a little thing. But I followed the doctor's orders and spent the entire day on the couch, doing nothing.

I was not built for that bullshit.

All I thought about all day was Gabbi and what she said. I still can't figure out what the hell I did to Hollie that pissed Gabbi off. Or how Gabbi even knows Hollie, for that matter. But I'd very much like to know the answers to both of those questions.

"Yeah, his brain is fine," Devlin Ramsey says. "The puck didn't get anywhere near his pinky toe."

I flip him off behind my back as the rest of the team laughs, the assholes. They give me a lot of shit—only a crazy man willingly plays goalie—but they all know I'm a smart motherfucker. I may be feral, but my mama didn't raise no fool.

I just happen to think life is too goddamn short to take everything seriously. We bust our asses day in and day out, pushing ourselves to the breaking point for a sport we love. If we can't have fun while playing it, what's the fucking point of any of it?

We head to our booth at the back of Park Avenue Bar, the only bar in town where people don't bug the shit out of us. Bender and Razor Montgomery are partial owners of the bar, both of whom are literal rockstars. When the owners of the place are infinitely more famous than your entire team, you tend not to make waves.

It's a nice change from the norm. Since the team moved to town, we've been creating waves everywhere we go. Billionaires are schmoozy people. They're also fucking sharks.

If I had a quarter for every time one tried to talk me into becoming their new spokesperson, doing an ad for their company, posing with a product on social media, or endorsing whatever they're hocking, I'd have a whole lot of quarters. So would every other man on the team.

I stumble halfway through the bar and nearly collide with Evie, the middle-aged bartender.

She tsks at me and then winks before sliding around us with her tray of drinks.

"Your ass should be at home in bed," Jensen Sparks says with a disapproving shake of his head. "You damn near got knocked out yesterday."

"It'll take more than Miles with a stick to knock his big ass out," Colter mutters, waving over Razor Montgomery's wife, Adalynn, once we reach our booth.

"Try harder next time," Reid tells Miles.

"You're all assholes." I glare at them. "If you lose tomorrow, it'll serve your asses right."

Reid's face falls. "Chuck is a fucking disaster in the net."

Chuck Willie, our backup goalie, is a disaster in the net. The man needs glasses and a miracle. His lateral movement and glove hand are shit.

"We'll just have to keep them away from the net then," Miles says, his expression grim. "It's going to be a long two weeks."

Colter and Jensen both nod glumly.

"Hey, guys," Adalynn says a few seconds later, stopping beside the table. She looks frazzled. "You want your usual beer and nachos?"

"I'll take water." I think about it for a moment, my stomach churning at the thought of bar food. "And skip the nachos for me."

Everyone at the table turns to look at me with matching expressions. Even Adalynn lifts a brow in surprise, but she doesn't comment. As soon as she walks away, Noah narrows his eyes on me.

"You need to go the fuck home and go back to bed, brother. You look like shit, and you just willingly skipped food."

"Can't a motherfucker just not be hungry?"

"No," everyone says at the exact same time.

"Man, fuck y'all," I mutter. I'm not even mad, though. Truth is...they're right. I should have my big ass at home in bed. My head is pounding, and the roar of noise here isn't helping. Neither are the stage lights.

"If by *fuck y'all*, you mean thank you, then you're welcome," Reid smirks at me. "Take your big ass home before you do more damage to your brain, and we get stuck with Chuck for the rest of the season."

"Yeah, I'm going." I haul myself out of the booth, scowling at them. "Later, fuckers."

"Later."

I weave my way through the bar, shaking my head. They're assholes, but I'm glad we ended up on the same team. They could have all been like Chuck. When new teams form, you never know what you're going to get. The league picks and chooses from every team, assigning players at random. We ended up with a solid roster.

Halfway to the door, a woman emerges from the hallway leading to the bathrooms just as I pass by. She's got her head down, walking fast. I try to dodge her, but there's no stopping the inevitable collision.

She slams right into me, bouncing off my chest with an oomph of sound.

"Shit, sorry." I grab for her to keep her from landing on her ass on the bar floor.

"I'm so sorry!" a sweet voice says at the same time.

I immediately recognize her voice.

"Gabbi." I look her over, my dick stiffening when I realize it really is her. Unlike yesterday, she isn't dressed for the Arctic now. She's in a tight black dress that's far too short, her hair hanging in loose waves around her face. Her eyes are dark and smoky. She looks like pure sex.

My dick agrees. He presses against my zipper hard enough to leave indentions along my shaft. Jesus Christ. She's a knockout.

"What the fuck are you wearing?" I growl, not sure if I'm more turned on or pissed that she's here alone, looking like the sweetest temptation.

"What?" She blinks long, sooty lashes at me, clearly confused by the question.

"Your dress is missing about eight inches."

She glances down at herself and then back up at me. "No, it isn't." Her lips purse. "Can you please let go of me now?"

Hell no.

I reluctantly release her.

We stare at each other in silence for a long moment.

"What are you doing here?" I ask her.

"How's your head?" she asks at the same time.

"Meeting Jordan."

"Fine."

"You probably shouldn't be at a bar with a concussion."

"What did Hollie say about me?"

Her entire demeanor changes when I ask the question. She goes from tolerating me to pissed off little kitten in the blink of an eye. "Are you kidding me right now, Atlas? You slept with her, broke her heart, and you're worried about what she said about you?" She eyes me like I'm the biggest disappointment she's ever met in her life. "That's just...I don't know what that is, but it's gross."

"Slept with her? What the fuck are you talking about? I've never slept with Hollie." I've never slept with anyone, let alone with our physical therapist. I may be the biggest virgin in the AHL, literally. Wherever she's getting her information from, she's getting bad information.

"Oh, so you're calling my best friend a liar?" She slams her hands down on her hips, scowling at me.

"Hold on. *Hollie* is your best friend?"

"Yes."

"And she told you that we slept together?"

"Obviously. She's not a puck bunny, you big jerk. She was a virgin. It's really messed up that you waited to end it until after you slept with her when the two of you work together."

Jesus fucking Christ. No wonder she hates me. She thinks I took her best friend's virginity and then ditched her. I'd hate me too if it were true. Unfortunately for me, it's not. And unfortunately for me, I'm not sure the truth means a damn thing right now.

Of course, she's going to believe her best friend over me. She doesn't even know me.

Our physical therapist just sank any hope I had before I even knew this gorgeous little pixie existed.

What the fuck?

CHAPTER THREE

Gabbi

Atlas stares at me with soulful green eyes, not saying anything for a long moment. It's unfortunate that he's a jerk because he's hot as Hades. The man towers over me like a freaking mountain casting a shadow. It's not hard to see why they put him in the goal when he's as big as he is.

I know from listening to Jordan that he's talented too. The only reason he isn't in the NHL is because he got into trouble last time he was called up. Apparently, he's kind of a crazy person.

Based on what I've seen of him, it tracks.

I'm not sure why I'm so disappointed that he slept with Hollie Janara, my best friend. I don't even know him. But I'm not just mad that he broke her heart. I'm disappointed with *him*, as if he personally harmed me. It makes no sense. But I haven't been able to get him off my mind since I saw him at the arena yesterday.

I haven't been able to stop thinking about the fact that he slept with Hollie, either.

It's driving me crazy.

"Do you have Hollie's number, Gabbi?" he asks, leaning close to ensure I hear him over the roar of the bar. The place is packed. Then again, Bender's bar usually is when they're putting on a show. Since the band retired, it's the only place they play anymore.

I was supposed to meet Roman and Jordan—my brothers—here to negotiate Christmas plans, but they both bailed on me. I think they're trying to avoid discussing the holiday yet again. They do it every year. I don't know why they're such Grinches.

"Why?"

"I'd like to speak to her."

"I'm not giving out her number, Atlas."

"Fine. Then will you step outside with me and call her so I can speak with her?"

I eye him warily, not sure what he's up to, but not entirely sure I trust him, either. "Why do you want to talk to her?"

"To clarify a few things."

"Like what?"

"Like why she told you that I slept with and dumped her when we've never even dated."

Technically, she didn't tell me that he dumped her. I worked that part out for myself. Three days ago, I came home to find her sobbing on the couch. I could barely get her to tell me what happened, but she finally admitted that she was in love with someone and had slept with him, but that it was over. Getting a name out of her took everything short of an Act of Congress.

She's been miserable. It's breaking my heart for her, but she refused to confront him. So I asked Jordan if I could tag along to the arena because I intended to do it for her. I didn't expect him to get hit in the head with a puck, though. My whole plan kind of went out the window at that point.

But the universe put us in the same place tonight, so I'm seizing the moment. I can't unbreak her heart, but I can give this giant a piece of my mind on her behalf. Maybe he'll think twice before doing the same thing to some other poor girl in the future.

My stomach twists, something curiously like jealousy shooting through me at the thought of him with some other girl. No, it's not jealousy. It *can't* be jealousy.

Get it together, Gabbi.

"She's not a liar, Atlas."

"I'm not saying she is, beautiful. But there's been some kind of misunderstanding here that I'd very much like to clear up, considering that I've never slept with anyone, let alone our physical therapist. I don't shit where I eat," he says bluntly.

"*You're* a virgin?"

"Yes," he states calmly, as if it doesn't bother him at all to admit it. "I don't know what your brother told you, but not all hockey players sleep around, Temptation."

My brother didn't tell me anything. He'd prefer if we never discussed his players or anyone with a penis, for that matter. As far as he's concerned, I'll never be old enough to date. It's annoying, really. But he's been involved in the sports world for most of my life. I know how it is.

And it doesn't take a rocket scientist to figure out that men who look like Atlas have options. A *lot* of options. Women have been going crazy for him and his teammates since they moved to town a few months ago. Hollie says that over half the fans packing the arena are women. Most aren't there because they have a vested stake in hockey. They show up because they have an interest in the men playing the sport.

He could crook his finger and they'd fall at his feet. There's no freaking way he's still a virgin, and yet...and yet, there's nothing but earnest honesty peeping out of those seafoam green eyes. He genuinely expects me to believe that he's a virgin.

"Hollie wouldn't lie," I say again, refusing to believe it. She's been my best friend since our freshman year of college. We do everything together, tell each other everything. She's one of the most genuine, honest people I know.

"Call her, Gabbi."

I hesitate for a brief moment, wavering. "I'll talk to her," I say instead. "If she wants to talk to you, I'll give her your number."

"Fine." He holds his hand out.

I eye it suspiciously, which makes him smile.

"I need your phone, Temptation."

"Oh. Right." I reluctantly drag it from my pocket and then hesitate before dropping it into his hand.

He looks at the case and then quirks a brow at me, his smile growing.

"Shut up," I mumble, refusing to be ashamed of my glittery purple and teal case. It's over-the-top bright and ridiculous with rhinestones around the edges, but I never lose my dang phone anymore.

"You need a password, beautiful. Your banking app is on this thing."

I gasp and grab for it, but he holds it over my head. "Stop looking at my stuff!"

"Put a password on your phone, baby."

My stomach flip-flops. I scowl daggers at him. "*Don't* call me that."

"You only hate it because you think I slept with your best friend," he murmurs, his fingers flying across my phone screen. "As soon as we clear this shit up, you'll melt every time I say it, Temptation."

"No, I won't. I mean, we aren't going to be clearing this up because you're lying."

He smirks at me, holding my phone out. By the time I slip it back into my bra, he's scowling. "Here." He shrugs out of his coat, stumbling in the process. His face pales slightly. Only then do I notice the pain swimming in his eyes.

"You need to go home, Atlas. You have a concussion," I whisper, softening toward him slightly. I can't help it. Seeing people in pain makes me sad. That's precisely why I went into nursing even though my brothers are both freaking billionaires who think I should sit at home and let them take care of me all day.

"I'm going." He steps forward, slipping his jacket around my shoulders. It settles over me like a warm hug, wrapping me in his spicy scent. "Wear this before you get me banned from my favorite bar."

"Atlas," I start to protest, but he's already weaving his way through the tables, heading toward the entrance.

I watch him go, conflicted and confused and not at all sure what the heck just happened.

"I had the strangest night," Hollie says as soon as I walk through the front door of our two-bedroom apartment. She's curled up on the sectional in her PJs, a fluffy blanket thrown over her lap. An episode of Supernatural plays on the TV. She seems...happy. Happier than she has been all week, anyway.

Did she lie about Atlas? Why would she? It just doesn't make sense.

"You tell me about yours, I'll tell you about mine," I say, kicking my shoes off and tossing my keys in the bowl on the console table before I collapse beside her on the sofa.

"I found a dog in my bed." She lays her dark head against mine, tossing her blanket across my lap. "A literal dog."

"What?" I turn to look at her. "You're serious?"

She makes big eyes at me, nodding. "I go in there with my boobs out to change, and there's this little fluffy white dog just sitting in the middle of the bed like, *Hello, nice to meet you. I, too, have boobs.*"

I giggle, unable to help myself.

"She escaped from the new neighbor's apartment and came through my window, I guess. I thought I was seeing things. Once we stopped staring each other down like

What the frack, I put a shirt on and went in search of where she belonged." Hollie smiles, humor in her eyes. "Our new neighbor is Heidi, Adalynn Montgomery's sister. The dog is Daphne. She's an escape artist."

"How did she get through your window?"

"We have no idea!" Hollie cries. "She's like a foot tall and five pounds!"

"I would have peed myself if I walked in to find a dog in my bed."

"I almost did. She was just sitting there, staring at my boobs like she owned the place."

I giggle again.

"Tell me about your night."

"It doesn't top yours," I say, suddenly reluctant to bring Atlas up at all. She's laughing and happy. I don't want to bring her crashing back down to earth. But something isn't adding up somewhere. Atlas was so convincing tonight. Is he really that good of a liar?

My heart tells me no. It also tells me Hollie isn't a liar either. What does that leave? I don't know.

"Tell me anyway. Did your brothers try to skip out on Christmas planning again?"

"They both skipped out on meeting up."

"Really?"

"I guess I'll just have to freaking ninja attack them with a Christmas tree and presents again." I shrug. "It worked last time."

"So what happened tonight?"

"I met Atlas," I admit quietly, watching her out of the corner of my eye to gauge her reaction. It might be my imagination, but it looks like she pales slightly. "Actually, I met him yesterday, but I saw him again tonight. He was at the bar with some of his teammates."

"Oh."

"I might have told him off."

"Gabbi, you didn't!"

"I did."

Tears spring to her eyes. She doesn't say anything. She doesn't have to say it. I've known her long enough to be able to read her like a book. The guilt in her eyes is crystal clear. She didn't sleep with Atlas.

"You lied to me."

"I'm sorry!" she cries. "You wanted a name and I panicked. His was on my roster for the day, so I just blurted it out. You're allergic to sports, so I didn't think you'd ever meet him."

"What? Why did you panic?" I press my palms to my cheeks, my mind reeling with mortification. I accused him of taking her virginity and then ghosting her. Oh my gosh. I was so mean to him!

"Be-because I don't want you to hate me," she whispers.

"Hollie." My face falls. "I could *never* hate you."

"You might when you know the truth." Her bottom lip quivers. "Maybe you should anyway. Atlas is a good guy.

I shouldn't have given you his name, but once it was out there, I didn't know how to take it back."

"I won't hate you," I promise. It's unfathomable how she could even think I ever could.

"I'm in love with your brother." Tears spill down her cheeks. "I've been in love with him since I met him, so I d-did something awful."

"What did you do?" I'm almost afraid to ask, but I'm not sure how it can get any worse.

"I slept with him at Roman's club. Only he doesn't know it was me. There was a masquerade party and we got carried away. I was going to tell him, but I was afraid he'd never forgive me. I just...freaked out so I ran."

My heart sinks. I was wrong. It *can* get worse.

"Oh, Hollie." I throw my arms around her, pulling her into a tight hug. I feel awful for not knowing she had a thing for Jordan. I've always suspected that he was into her. It's just the way he looks at her. But she's always been so shy and quiet around him. I can't even wrap my mind around the fact that they hooked up at Roman's club, The Sterling Rope. I can't even process that she *went* to Roman's club.

It's a BDSM club. I only know it exists because it was impossible for Roman and Jordan to hide it from me, but most of Silver Spoon Falls knows nothing about its existence. It's a closely guarded secret, held only by those who walk through the doors. My brother banned me from ever stepping foot inside. I guess the same rule doesn't apply to Hollie.

I didn't even know she *wanted* to go. It's like my best friend is this whole other person I never knew, one who takes big risks, even if they end in disaster. When have I ever done that? Never. I've always played it safe and done what was expected of me.

I'm disappointed that she lied to me. I'm disappointed that she thought she couldn't tell me the truth. But I'm not mad. I...envy her. She went after what she wanted. Maybe she didn't do it the right way. Maybe she made a mess of everything along the way, but she tried. That takes courage.

I've never had that.

"I could never hate you," I whisper fiercely.

She sobs on my shoulder. "Your b-brother is going to h-hate me when he f-finds out the truth."

Maybe. Maybe not. I don't know. Jordan is his own person. I think he's in love with Hollie and has been for a while, but he's never acted on it...unless he did. He has a rigid sense of right and wrong and a steadfast sense of loyalty. The fact that she's so much younger than he is and is my best friend probably weighs on him. But he hasn't been on a single date since he met her. Is it possible he knew who she was in the club?

I don't know.

All I know is that they need to work this out because I don't want to be caught in the middle of my best friend and my brother. I don't want to be stuck between two of the people I love most in this world, keeping secrets for both of them. My brothers mean the world to me. They've been my heroes for my entire life. But Hollie is the sister I always wanted.

"Talk to him, Hollie," I encourage her, knowing nothing will ever be solved if she doesn't confess. "You owe it to yourself and to him."

"I will," she sniffles. "Eventually."

I sigh, deciding not to push. She made a huge mistake, but she's one of the best people I know. She'll make the right decision in due time.

"How mad is Atlas?" she asks after a moment, dabbing her eyes with the corner of the blanket. "Does he hate me?"

"I think he's more confused than mad."

"I'm such a jerk."

"If you're a jerk, I'm a bigger jerk." I cringe. "I basically verbally assaulted him."

"What did you say?"

"Don't ask."

"What did *he* say?"

"He gave me his coat and told me to put a password on my phone."

"Oh." Her eyes grow wide. "He likes you."

"What? No, he doesn't."

"Oh my gosh! You like him too!"

"What?" I rapidly shake my head, denying it. "I don't."

"You do. It's written all over your face. You like him."

"I do," I groan, admitting it to her and to myself. I hide my face in my hands, my cheeks hot as the truth washes through me. I do like him. More than I should. "I so do!"

She laughs quietly. "Good for you. He's a good guy. Um, a little crazy."

"Yeah, I'm getting that." I drag my hands away from my face, peeking over at her. "He says the most ridiculous things." Like telling me I'd melt when he called me baby. Or asking where the rest of my dress is. Or telling me that his balls hurt. I'm pretty sure he knew exactly what he was saying yesterday, but he said it anyway. He's ridiculous, and I kind of love it.

"You're blushing."

I sigh. "It doesn't matter if I like him or not. Jordan owns the team. He'll kill us both. And Roman will help." They're both overprotective to a fault. I've never dated because it's virtually impossible when your brothers are billionaires with unlimited resources at their fingertips.

The one—and only—time I told them I got asked out, they had his entire life story in five minutes flat and threatened to send me to a convent if I even thought about going out with him simply because he'd been arrested once for public intoxication. He got drunk on Spring Break when he was eighteen.

Hollie's face falls, but she doesn't disagree with my assessment.

CHAPTER FOUR

Gabbi

I wait until Hollie is in bed to text Atlas to apologize. Except he didn't put himself in my phone as Atlas. He listed himself as my future husband. He even added himself to my emergency contacts.

He's shameless, really.

I shake my head, a stupid smile on my face as I set it aside to crawl into my bed. I settle against the pillows, dragging my fuchsia Patina Vie duvet up over my lap. Once I'm snuggled in, I grab my phone again to type out a quick text.

> **Me:** Did you seriously add yourself to my emergency contacts?

> Not My Future Husband: Who me?

> Me: Yes, you.

> Not My Future Husband: IDK. I guess people can do anything when you DON'T HAVE A PASSWORD ON YOUR PHONE.

> Me: Don't shouty caps me.

> Not My Future Husband: Do you like my name?

> Me: You mean this one?

I take a quick screenshot of the change I made to his entry and send it to him.

> Me: Love it. Very accurate.

Two seconds later, my phone rings.

I hesitate long enough for him to send another text.

> Not My Future Husband: Answer the phone, Temptation.

I swipe to answer. "Don't tell me what to do, Atlas."

"You changed my name in your contacts."

"Who, me? I guess anyone can do anything when they own the phone."

He growls at me. And wow. I didn't know men actually did that in real life. Or that it'd sound so menacing and hot at the same time. Coming from him, it's both. A shiver works its way through me.

Crap. He's working hockey hunk voodoo on me.

I shake my head hard, trying to dispel it so I can focus.

"We aren't getting married, Atlas. I don't even know you."

"You will," he says confidently. "I'll tell you anything you want to know."

Oh, really?

"What did you do to get sent down from the NHL?"

"I sent a bag of dicks and a glitter bomb to the owner of the team."

"What?" I laugh in shock. "Are you serious?"

"As a heart attack."

"Why?"

"He nixed fighting a suspension for a teammate that never should have happened. It was a bad call, so I let him know how we felt about it. I guess he didn't feel like eating a bag of dicks that day."

I choke on laughter, clamping a hand over my mouth. "You're terrible."

"I'm honest, Temptation. It wasn't my first time pissing in his Cheerios. I'm not someone who goes along quietly. He didn't like that, so I got sent down."

"You are honest," I whisper.

"You talked to Hollie."

"I did." I take a deep breath. "I'm woman enough to admit when I'm wrong, and I was wrong. I'm sorry I called you an oversized manwhore."

"You didn't call me an oversized manwhore."

"I did in my head." I pause. "A lot. Like a *lot*."

He laughs quietly at the way I draw out the word. "I've been called worse."

"I'm also sorry I called you a jerk and accused you of lying."

"That one you did say out loud." He chuckles and then sobers. "You believe me now?"

"Yes. Um, she told me what really happened."

"Care to share?"

It's not really my business to share her business, but I figure I owe him a few answers at this point, so I give him the Cliff Notes version. "She's in love with my brother. Things got spicy between them. She didn't know how to tell me."

"Ah, I see."

"Please don't get her fired," I plead quietly. "She only used your name because she was afraid to tell me the truth, and your name was the first one that came to mind. She didn't know I was going to confront you. She didn't think I'd ever even meet you. Had she known, she never would have given me your name. She feels awful."

"I'm not interested in going after her job, Temptation. I'm interested in something else."

"W-what?"

"You," he growls.

"Atlas."

"I saw the way you looked at me before you remembered you were supposed to hate me, baby. You felt the same spark zinging through your body that had my cock ready to burst. I know you did."

I did feel it, but I don't tell him that. I don't say anything.

"I couldn't tell through that fucking parka you had on, but I'm guessing it had those little nipples hard and your panties soaked, didn't it?" he rasps.

I bite my lip, fighting the urge to admit the truth.

"Didn't it, Temptation?"

"Yes," I whisper. In the moments before I remembered why I couldn't like him, I felt an avalanche move through me, twisting me all up and putting me back together in some new order. My body ached for something I've never had...the same way it aches right now. I want this man in a way I've never wanted anything.

That scares me. It excites me. It frustrates and annoys me. I don't want to like him. I don't want to want him. I *can't* because what was true in the living room earlier is just as true now. My brother still owns the team he plays for. He's already gotten booted from the NHL by an irate owner. What happens if Jordan decides he wants him off the Falcons?

Many AHL players don't have the same temporary permanency that NHL players do. Once an NHL player is on a team, it takes a lot of jumping through hoops to move them before their contract is up or the season ends. For an AHL player like Atlas, all it takes is a phone call, and they're on a plane, loaned to another team, even if it's the middle of a season.

I don't want Jordan to make that call for Atlas in some misguided attempt to protect me. I'm twenty-two, old enough to make my own choices. But our parents died when I was four, leaving Jordan to raise me. Convincing him to see me as a capable, functional adult instead of the little girl who needed him to slay the monsters under her bed is far easier said than done.

"Fuck," Atlas groans. "Now you've got my dick playing the obedient little soldier again. He's standing at attention for you."

I squeeze my thighs together, fighting a whimper.

"Come to practice with me tomorrow, Temptation. When I get back from New Mexico, I'll take you out, and we'll get to know each other."

I want to say yes. So freaking bad.

"I can't," I whisper instead. "My brother."

"Shit. Then skip practice and agree to go out with me when I get home."

"No, Atlas. I mean I can't, period. He owns the team." Disappointment fills me, as if I'm the one being rejected here. If he weren't a hockey player, I'd say yes in a heartbeat. But I can't risk his career because my brother is a crazy person.

"I'm not afraid of your brother, Gabbi."

"Well, you should be," I say bluntly. "He controls your fate so long as you're on his team. And if I go out with you, you'll be on a plane to a team on the other side of the country before the ink even dries on the paperwork."

"Let me worry about Jordan. I can handle him, Temptation."

"He's my brother. He raised me. Trust me, Atlas. If we go out, there will be no *handling* him. I'm sorry, but no. I need to go."

"I'm not going to give up," he growls. "I know you want me, baby. I'm not going to quit pursuing you until you're mine; that's a promise."

"It sounds more like a threat," I mutter, pouting about it even though I kind of like the thought of him refusing to give up easily. There's never been anyone who wanted to fight for me before. The fact that this man wants to do it is sweet. I didn't expect that from him.

"Nah, Temptation. If you wear that fucking dress out again, I'm going to cut it from your body and tie you up with the scraps while I fuck you," he says, his voice dark. "*That's* a threat. If you run, I'll chase. When I catch you,

I'll make you pay for running while you're riding my face. *That's* a promise. See the difference?"

Good grief. They both sound like a good time to me. For a virgin, he has a filthy mouth and an inventive imagination. He probably also has the confidence to follow through on everything he just said. His arrogance should be a turn-off, but it's having the opposite effect on me. I love it a little too much.

There's nothing shy or awkward or hesitant about this man. He may be a virgin like he said, but he may also be the most capable one I've ever met. I am not nearly that self-assured or self-possessed. Just thinking about saying any of the stuff he just said makes me squirm.

Where did this man come from? And what God do I have to pray to in order to keep him? Asking for a friend. Obviously.

"I have to go," I sigh. "Goodnight, Atlas."

"Night, baby. Dream of me."

As if there's any doubts about that happening.

I toss and turn half the night, unable to get comfortable or shut my mind off. My body aches—which is entirely his fault. Halfway through the night, I slip my hand inside my panties and try to get myself off.

I call up a fantasy of him. His words replay in my mind. I see his seafoam green eyes boring into me, commanding me to come. But it's as if my body refuses to get there. No matter how hard I try, I just can't finish.

I finally give up and cover my face with a pillow, groaning in frustration.

He hasn't even touched me, and he's already ruined me.

Eventually, exhaustion pulls me under. The crazy goalie haunts my sleep. In my dreams, he does the filthiest things to me. I'm tied to the goal while he cuts my favorite dress from my body. Even though the ice is cold, I don't feel the chill. I'm a bundle of raw nerves and hungry flame, tangled in the possessive desire in his eyes.

My alarm jolts me awake before we get to the good part. I groan, thrashing around on the bed in what I'm not ashamed to admit is a minor tantrum. I can't even get off in my sleep. This sucks.

I'm still trying to pull myself together when my phone dings with an incoming message. I grab it, hoping that it's Atlas.

It's Jordan.

Big Brother: Before you ignore me, this is important.

I ignore him anyway. He stood me up yesterday. I'm mad at him.

> Big Brother: I'm serious, Half-Pint.

If him and Roman don't stop calling me that, I may kill them both. I swear, they think it's hilarious to make fun of me for being short. As if it's my fault they got the tall gene, and I didn't.

> Me: You always say that.

> Big Brother: I mean it this time.

I decide to hear him out, curious if he's going to confess to sleeping with Hollie. Surely he knows it was her. He has to know...right?

> Me: Fine. What do you want?

> Big Brother: Breakfast. Are you hungry?

I stare at his text for a long moment and then smile despite myself. Of course that's what he wants. He hates when I'm mad at him. It drives him crazy.

Me: Breakfast isn't important, Jordan.

Big Brother: It's the most important meal of the day, Half-Pint. Meet me at the diner in an hour.

Me: Fine. But I'm still mad at you.

Big Brother: I know.

By the time I get to the 5th Avenue Diner, Jordan is already at our booth in the left corner. Why the place is called a diner, I don't know. It was recently remodeled and is seriously nice, like it was plucked straight from a bygone era. The burnished gold floor and plush red booths give it a luxurious vibe that's almost commonplace in this town.

Nothing here is ever simple. Everything is posh and elegant, designed to make the rich men who call this town home at ease.

Like usual, the place is packed full of men in suits, drinking coffee as they peruse Wall Street Journal or chat with associates over breakfast.

"I ordered your usual for you," Jordan murmurs, rising to his feet to meet me.

"With extra whipped cream?"

"Do I look like I want to die?" He smirks, dropping a kiss on my forehead. "Of course, I ordered extra whipped cream."

"Good. I guess I'll let you live."

He chuckles, waiting for me to slide into the booth before he sits opposite me, one arm thrown across the back of the bench. "So you're still mad?"

I hold my finger and thumb a fraction of an inch apart. "You and Roman both stood me up."

"Roman ditched your Come to Jesus too?"

"Ha! At least you admit you ditched."

He shrugs, unrepentant. "I had shit to do, Half-Pint."

"Like what?'

"Shit." He waves me off. "But I'm here now. So let's hear it."

"You can't work through Christmas this year. I forbid it," I say, crossing my arms to glare at him. "Roman either. We're having a traditional Christmas like a normal family, and you are both going to be there."

"We aren't a normal family."

I grimace at the reminder. I guess when you lose your parents in a fiery plane crash two days before Christmas, there isn't a lot to celebrate. He and Roman are both old enough to remember losing our parents, but I don't even remember them. I was only four when their plane went down.

But I think it's important to celebrate the holiday even if we aren't normal. My brothers need a reminder that there is more to life than work. God knows, if it were up to them, they'd spend all day, every day at their respective offices. They need to live a little.

"No family is normal, Jordan," I say quietly. "Every family looks different. It doesn't make them any less of a functional, cohesive family. You've worked through Christmas every year since I started college. I miss you."

His expression softens. "I haven't gone anywhere, Half-Pint."

"Good. Then it won't be a problem for us to have Christmas at your place." I beam at him, batting my lashes. "Unless you and Rome want to carry a giant tree up three flights of stairs to mine and Hollie's apartment."

He goes still as soon as I say her name. "Is she spending Christmas with us again this year?"

"Yes," I say slowly. Hollie's parents are...honestly, I don't know what to call her parents. As soon as she graduated from high school, they sold their house and all their worldly possessions and took up cruising the world. Last I heard, they were in Iceland. Hollie spends most holidays with us as a result.

Jordan nods slowly. "Fine. We'll do Christmas at the house. I'll even buy a damn tree for you two to decorate."

I fight the urge to gape at him, stunned at how quickly he capitulated. Does he know the woman he met at Rome's masquerade party was Hollie, or is he just trying to appease me? I don't know!

Our food arrives before I can work it out. My stomach growls as I dig into my strawberry crepes heaped with whipped cream.

Jordan watches me in amusement, shaking his head. "That shit still doesn't qualify as breakfast, Half-Pint."

"Shut up," I mumble around a mouthful.

We eat in silence for a few moments before I work up the nerve to bring up Atlas...and by *bring him up* I mean I lie like the wind.

"How is the hockey player that got hit with the puck? Atlas, right?" Oh, I'm good, and I'm going to hell for it.

Forgive me, Baby Jesus.

"Out for two weeks." Jordan scowls at the reminder. "His replacement is shit."

"He can't play for two weeks?"

"We'll be lucky if he's only out that long," my brother mutters.

"What? Why?"

"This is his second concussion in a year. We're not taking it lightly. If we have to bench him for the rest of the season to ensure he's able to keep playing for as long as possible, that's what we'll do."

This is what I love about my brother. A lot of people would push for their players to return to the ice as soon as possible. How many times has one played through a head injury in a professional sport? Jordan isn't like that. For him, the players mean more than a win, even if it costs him now. He'd rather have a healthy player in the long run than a win in the short-term. He values people above business.

But it sucks for Atlas. It's his first season with the Falcons, and it's only just begun.

"You like Atlas, don't you?" I ask softly.

"Wouldn't have pushed to get him signed to the team if I didn't." He narrows his eyes on me. "Why?"

"Just curious," I lie.

"Gabriella."

"What?"

"Don't bullshit me. Why are you asking?"

"I was just curious." I shrug. "Is that a crime?"

"Fuck yes," Jordan growls. "You aren't dating one of my players. Actually, you aren't dating at all. You're too young."

"I'm twenty-two, Jordan."

"Exactly. Too young."

"Hollie is only twenty-three." I purse my lips at him. "Are we going to pretend you don't like her?"

He eyes me levelly. "We aren't talking about Hollie. We're talking about you. You aren't dating Atlas Jacks. Don't even fucking think about it, Half-Pint."

"Oh my gosh!" I scowl at him. "Stop telling me what to do. Besides, I wasn't thinking about it. I was just asking how he was doing, considering he got hit in the head with a freaking puck right in front of me. I didn't know that was a crime. But maybe we should be talking about Hollie."

"There's nothing to talk about."

"You are so full of it." And I'm more convinced than ever that he's in love with my best friend. Unfortunately, I'm also more convinced than ever that he'd lose his mind if he knew the way Atlas talked to me on the phone last night.

Atlas wouldn't have to worry about the concussion ending his season. I'm pretty sure Jordan would do it on principal. If that happens, there may not be a future in the AHL for him. *That's* the kind of pull my brother has.

I can't let that happen.

CHAPTER FIVE

Atlas

"**C**heesus Thrist," I groan, reaching blindly for a pillow as the alarm clock screams like a banshee, far too early to be polite. My head pounds. My tongue feels cloven to the roof of my mouth. In short, I feel like I drank my weight in vodka last night. When you're as big as I am, it's a lot of fucking vodka.

Unfortunately for me, I didn't drink a single drop.

I'm lust-drunk, love-stoned, and sleep-deprived. My sweet little Temptation ran through my mind all fucking night, leaving my cock hard and aching. Sleeping with a steel rod between your legs is next to impossible.

My fingers close around the edge of a pillowcase. I hoist it, sending the soft missile whipping across the room toward my alarm clock. It slams into the table, sending everything on top crashing to the floor.

The alarm squawks one final time and goes blessedly silent.

Finally.

I drag the blanket back over my head. My eyes drift closed.

"Pick up the phone, your bro is calling you. Pick up the phone, your bro is calling you!" my phone sings. "Your phone, your phone, your bro is on the phone!"

I add a pillow to the blanket covering my head. Maybe if I suffocate and die, Coach will call off our game in New Mexico. Spending two days on a bus with our driver—who I'm not even convinced has a license to operate a Tonka truck, let alone a passenger bus—doesn't sound like a good time to me right now.

The phone stops...and immediately starts blaring again. Change of plans. I can't suffocate and die until I kill Colter for fucking with my phone. I know it was him. He's the only asshole on the team always messing with our shit.

Snatching the pillow off my head, I grab my phone and sit upright. My head swims as my skull plays ping-pong with my brain. I slap the screen of the phone to answer, pressing the speaker button.

"I hate you," I mutter. "It's too goddamn early for your shit, Colter."

"Good morning to you too, Sunshine," he says with a laugh.

"How are you functioning?"

"Uh, I don't have a concussion, and I didn't bet a professional bartender that I could outdrink her?"

"Who the fuck did that?"

"Devlin."

Well, now he's got my attention.

"Did he win?"

"She's in her late fifties, and she's been bartending she since was twenty-two. What do you think?"

Right, so he didn't win.

"Did he at least give her a run for her money?"

"Sure. If that's what you call hopping up on the bar, ripping his shirt off, and screaming that he's Batman immediately before falling off backward," he says, choking on laughter.

Jesus Christ. I'm almost sorry I missed it. Naw, not even a little bit. Spending the night on the phone with Gabbi while my dick was in my hand was infinitely more pleasurable than watching Devlin get drunk and act like an idiot. I see that shit every day of the week.

Talking to her is new. She's sweet as hell. If I can't figure out how to convince her to marry me immediately, I'm going to lose my shit. I need her in my life like I need air. She's vital to my survival now, the most necessary ingredient for sustaining life. I don't give a damn if her brother does own the team. Like I told her, I'm not afraid of him. She's a big girl, capable of making her own decisions. And I'm the best thing for her.

Jordan may not know it yet, but he will.

"Noah caught the whole thing on video." Colter cracks up again. "You better get your ass to the arena if you don't want him blaming you for passing it around. He said you owe him for that trip to Mexico."

Fuck my life. I'm never living down that trip. As if it's my fault Noah Diamante decided to go overboard with the tequila and thought letting Juan tattoo *Get Pucked* on his ass was a good idea. I tried to talk him out of it, but he's a persuasive motherfucker. Which is exactly how I ended up with a matching tattoo.

The goddamn puck is wearing a sombrero.

"I feel like I got hit by a truck," I mutter, scrubbing a hand down my face.

"That bad?"

"Worse." Every time I breathe, my head throbs. I know enough about concussions to know this isn't great news for my chances of returning to the ice anytime soon. Migraines after a concussion are never a good thing.

"Shit. You better get your ass in to see Jessup," Colter says, his voice somber.

"I'll call him from the road."

"It's your funeral."

"It'll be fine."

"Famous last words. See you when you get here."

"Later."

I disconnect, dropping the phone onto the bed beside me. There's no way I'm riding a bus to New Mexico like this, not today. Not with Keith driving the bastard. Which means I'm either staying behind, flying, or I'm driving solo. Considering I can't even see straight, I don't think I'll be driving anywhere, let alone to New Mexico.

Inspiration strikes like a fucking gong.

I pick up my phone and dial Gabbi's number.

"Hello?" she says breathlessly, answering on the fourth ring.

"I was worried you weren't going to answer," I admit, my cock twitching at the sound of her voice.

"I shouldn't have," she mutters, making me smile. She wants to resist me, but she can't. I fucking love knowing that.

"I'm glad you did, Temptation. I need a favor."

"What kind of favor? And if you tell me that you need me to go out with you, the answer is no, Atlas. That's not even a favor. It's called a date, and I already turned you down."

Christ, I love her sassy attitude. She doesn't take even an iota of shit from me. She's half my size and stands up to me like she's not in the least afraid. It's a hell of a turn-on. Most women who don't know me see me as a threat. And I get it. Women can't tell on sight who intends them harm and who doesn't, and a motherfucker built like me could do serious damage.

Until we teach all men respect, we have to continue to teach women to protect themselves by being cautious. It's how they stay safe. I don't begrudge them that. Shit, my heart goes out to them for it. It pisses me off that any woman has to live with that fear.

But I'm glad as hell Gabbi doesn't feel it when she looks at me. She trusts me instinctively, as if she knows that I'd kill for her before I let her come to any harm. As if she's never had to fear.

I'm guessing her brothers have worked their asses off to ensure she never had to fear anyone. I hope she retains that innocence for the rest of her life. When she's mine, I'll work my ass off to ensure she does.

"I need you to drive me to the game."

She goes completely silent.

"Temptation?"

"You mean the game in New Mexico?"

"That'd be the one."

"That isn't a favor, Atlas. That's insanity! It's a twelve-hour drive!"

"Eleven."

She harrumphs like I'm a crazy man, making me grin. Fuck, I can't wait until she's naked in my bed, giving me that attitude.

"It is a favor, baby," I say, trying to sway her to the Dark Side. "I have a concussion. I can't drive myself, and if I have to sit on a bus, I'll lose my mind."

"You have to have one to lose it, Atlas."

"If I'm out of my mind, it's only because you got me hit in the head with a puck."

"I got you hit?" she asks, incredulous. "How did I get you hit?"

"You walked into the arena, and I saw my future. You think I was thinking about where the goddamn puck was, Temptation? Fuck no. All I was thinking about was you. So yeah, you got me hit."

"You are so full of it," she says, but her voice is soft.

"I'm dead serious."

"Why not have one of your teammates drive you?"

"They aren't nurses. My head is fucking killing me, Temptation. I'm exhausted and dizzy as shit. I can't focus or walk a straight line."

"Atlas, you need to see your doctor again," she says softly, her worry evident. "You probably shouldn't be traveling at all."

"The team can't afford for your brother to bench me for the rest of the season, baby."

"Your health is more important than the game, Atlas." The disapproval in her voice comes through loud and clear. "There's always next season. But you can't undo permanent damage to your brain."

"I know, and I don't intend to cause permanent damage. I won't return before the Doc clears me," I promise. "But your brother is a hard ass when it comes to this shit. It's our first season. How we perform this season is critical for some of these guys. It's critical for determining whether there's a future for this team. If I'm out, it's going to seriously fuck things up."

Gabbi huffs in my ear, trying to convince me that she isn't buying what I'm selling, but I'm not lying to her. We've got a lot riding on this season. Contracts, who gets called up, how much the AHL invests in our success as a team...it all depends in part on how we perform. If I'm out all season and Chuck is in the net, we're all fucked.

"I'll be far better off with a nurse at my side than I would if I tried to make the trip without, Temptation."

"I'm not a nurse yet."

"You're working on your graduate degree in nursing. I think you're qualified."

"How do you know that?" she demands.

"Google."

"You Googled me?"

"I Googled the shit out of you. You look cute as hell on the 'Gram."

"Oh my god. Stop stalking my social media!"

"Uh, hell no. Have you seen how hot you are?"

"You're impossible."

"I wouldn't have to be if you'd say yes already." She knows I'm not just talking about this trip. I'm talking about us. I know she's on the verge of giving in to all of it. She's just afraid to take the leap and see where it leads.

I appreciate that she's trying to look out for my career, but I don't need her to protect me. I can handle myself. The only thing she needs to worry about is doing what makes her happy. I have a feeling she hasn't done much of that in her life. She worries too much about everyone else. I've known her for two days, and I know that much about her.

She loves fiercely and defends the people who matter to her like a little mama bear. I'm guessing she's done it her entire life, putting everyone else first. Doing what she was supposed to do to keep her brothers from worrying.

It's time for her to take a leap and live for herself.

"I'll pay for everything, including separate hotel rooms if you'd prefer to have your own," I say, trying to sweeten the deal. "All you have to do is drive."

"Is this even allowed?" she demands.

"Of course, it's allowed," I say, technically not lying to her. Coach may not be thrilled, but there's no rule preventing it. The way I see it, I have two days to convince her that she wants to be mine, despite her brother. If she doesn't agree, I'm going to her brother regardless of what she has to say.

The chips will fall where they will then. Either I'll be blackballed, and he'll no longer be my boss...or he'll kill me, and it won't matter. Maybe it's the concussion talking, but it seems to me like taking two days to try to convince her to fall for me before I fight fire with fire seems like the safest bet.

Her brother may be overprotective, but I doubt he'd kill me if doing it would make her unhappy. So I just need to make sure it'll make her unhappy.

What better way than spending two days locked in a car with her, destroying her defenses?

It's a genius plan, really. Concussed me may be the smartest me yet.

"Fine," she says. "But just so we're clear, this isn't a date. I'm only agreeing because you need someone to make sure you don't freaking die on the trip."

"You're doing what?" Coach says an hour later, his arms crossed as he stares at me like I've lost my damn mind.

"Riding to the game with Gabbi Sterling."

His silence is deafening. And then he laughs abruptly. "Jesus Christ, Jacks. If you weren't this ballsy all the time, I'd be worried. Sterling is going to murder you when he finds out."

"I fully intend to tell him."

"Oh, really?" Coach G smirks. "Then you'll be happy to know he's upstairs."

Fuck. I planned to call him, not discuss it face to face. Less chance of us coming to blows if we're not in the same room.

"Great," I say with false enthusiasm. "I'll just run up there now."

"The hell you will. The last thing we need is for him to try to knock your ass out when you already have a concussion." Coach G shakes his head, dragging his phone from his pocket. "I'll handle it."

"You aren't going to argue?"

"Would it do me any good?" He cocks a brow at me, waiting for me to shake my head before he speaks again. "That's what I thought." He sighs. "I thought they were bullshitting about the water in this town, but after the last few months, I'm starting to second-guess myself. The whole team will be married by the end of the season at this rate."

"What's wrong with the water in town?"

"Apparently, it's...You know what? It doesn't even matter. It's already too late for you."

"Well, that sounds ominous."

"Love is never ominous." He points to the chair across from his desk. "Sit your overgrown ass down before you collapse. I'll call Jordan."

"You're a good dude, Grayson."

"Oh, I'm not doing this out of the kindness of my heart, Jacks. I happen to like spending time with my wife. If you and Sterling are at each other's throats, I can't do that. And that'll piss me off, Jacks. She smells better than you assholes."

I drop heavily into the indicated chair, chuckling. I downed a few over-the-counter pain relievers on my way in. They've taken the edge off the headache, but I still feel like hammered shit.

"Sterling, you got a minute?" Coach G asks as soon as Jordan picks up his phone.

"What's up, Grayson?"

"Your sister is driving Jacks to New Mexico."

"What the fuck?" Jordan growls.

"Jacks can't travel with us, and I don't trust him to get himself to New Mexico without causing a fucking problem. He's a pain in my ass."

I lift my head to scowl at him, but he just shrugs as if to say it's true. Which is fair. I am a pain in his ass.

"He's still having symptoms. Since your sister is a nurse, she'll be babysitting him on the way to and from New Mexico."

"Are you asking me or telling me, Grayson?"

"Telling. You own the team, but when it comes to the day-to-day, I'm the one who has the make the calls down here on the ground," he says bluntly. "This is the right call. It'll keep him out of trouble and ensure we can keep an eye on him. Otherwise, we have to leave him behind."

He doesn't have to spell out that leaving me behind means everyone starts asking questions about the severity of my injury. That'll make sponsors nervous. Jordan is a smart man. He knows we need to play the injury down and keep sponsors happy. Like I told Gabbi, too much rides on this season. Jordan knows it as much as anyone else. More, perhaps. It's his money on the line.

"Son of a bitch," he curses. "Is Jacks there with you?"

"He is."

"Let me talk to him."

"You're on speaker."

"Jacks, if you put your hands on my sister, they'll be retrieving pieces of your body from here to the arena in Carson."

I could go along quietly. That's what I should do. But I'm not going to lie to the man. I'm playing for keeps here.

"With all due respect, what happens between your sister and me is between us, Sterling," I say. "I respect that you've been protecting her for most of her life, but you don't have to protect her from me. She's perfectly safe with me."

"She's got a degree to focus on," he growls.

"And I won't stand in her way. But she's capable of calling the shots in her own life. Trust her enough to let her do it, Sterling. You know she has killer instincts and is more than capable of putting me in my place if I need it."

"Keep your hands to yourself if you want to keep them," Jordan growls. "I'm not fucking around, Jacks."

"Neither am I. I'm going to marry your sister."

"Jesus H. Christ," Coach G mutters under his breath.

CHAPTER SIX

Gabbi

"You told my brother that we're getting married?" I whisper-shout at Atlas as soon as I fling open my front door to find him leaning against the balcony railing. "Are you insane?"

His green eyes rove over me, a smirk on his face. Despite his expression, it's obvious that he's exhausted and in pain. A fine sheen of pain coats his eyes, tightening his expression "I thought you concluded earlier today that I am crazy, Temptation."

"Clearly!" I cry, staring at him like he's a foreign species. I think he may be. There is no one else on the planet like this wild man. "He's been threatening to send me to a convent for the last two hours because of you."

"Yeah? You'd make a hell of a nun. Might even give me a fetish." His eyes dance over me again, darkening. "If he thinks a habit, a remote location, and a few devout old ladies would keep me from getting to you, he's wrong, though. I'd fuck you up against a wall in a convent, lick-ety-split."

"Oh, my god. Stop talking!" I feel the heat blazing like the sun in my cheeks. Does he ever say anything normal or is everything that comes out of his mouth shameless and filthy? I'm not sure I want to know the answer to that question.

He pushes away from the railing, grabbing for me.

Before I can even think to evade him, he's got his arms around me, dragging me up against his chest. For a man with a concussion, he moves quick. I melt into him without meaning to do it, my body pressed to his as if it's exactly where I belong. Electricity hums against my skin everywhere we touch, as if it's collecting there, preparing to unleash in a shower of lightning.

"Fuck," he growls, backing me up against the wall beside the door. "I planned on being a gentleman but that sassy fucking mouth of yours is ruining my plans, Temptation."

"Liar," I breathe. We both know he had no intention of being a gentleman. We both know that he's going to use every trick in the book to break through my defenses while we're on the road together. I knew it before I even agreed to drive him, but I agreed anyway. Because that's the power this man has over me. Because that's how crazy he makes me.

"Not lying," he says, brushing his nose against mine. His minty breath is wreaking havoc on my senses. Or maybe that's his cologne. Or the fact that I feel his erection against my belly. Or the fact that he's got his arms around me as if I belong to him. Perhaps it's all of the above. But I'm having trouble remembering why this shouldn't happen. "I did plan to be a gentleman. When I'm inside you, you'll come first. That's downright saintly, Temptation. Because I already know I'm not going to last for shit."

"Who says I'm going to sleep with you?"

His lips skim across the side of my face. "That soaked pussy says it, Gabbi," he growls against my ear. "You can lie to yourself about why you agreed to this trip, but we both know you said yes because you're fucking dying to feel me inside you."

"Atlas," I groan. It's supposed to be a warning for him to shut up. It comes out more like a needy plea for him to keep talking.

"Fuck." He draws the word out as if he's in pain. "You can't say my name like that if you don't want to give your neighbors a show." His lips settle against the side of my throat. Either my heart stops or it starts beating for the first time ever. I'm not sure. But I feel him as if he's laying a brand on my soul.

My head spins, all the reasons we can't do this threatening to drift away. In this moment, the fact that he could lose his career doesn't seem like such a big obstacle. His lips are against my skin and it's the closest to God I've ever come.

"Jesus Christ, Temptation. You're going to ruin me, aren't you?"

Probably. Just like he's going to ruin me. I think I knew it the moment I set eyes on him. I fought it because I thought he was someone he wasn't. But I knew if I let him close, he'd change my life. He's barely even entered it, and it's already upending everything, turning my neatly ordered life to chaos. And I don't hate it at all.

I feel braver and freer since I met him than I've ever felt.

"Yeah, you are," he says when I don't answer, seeking my lips with his. I think he intends the kiss to be a sweet punctuation to his statement. But it's anything but. As soon as his tongue touches my bottom lip, reality spirals away.

We end up locked in a heated embrace, kissing each other as if we've been separated by war. I lose track of everything except the way he possesses my mouth, coming back again and again to sip from my lips.

"Goddamn," he rasps, breaking away when a car door slams in the parking lot below. "Been waiting to do that since the arena."

I press my hot face to his throat, my mind reeling. I'm in way, way over my head with this man. And not even Jordan's threats are going to stop what's happening between us. It's far too late for that.

"Hell no," he growls thirty minutes later, staring at my Mercedes GT as if it just pooped on his carpet. "We're not taking your car."

"Yes, we are." I smirk at him. "I'm babysitting you. That makes me the boss of this trip. And the boss says we're taking my car. I adore my car. Rome bought it for me as a graduation present last year. It's small and flashy, but I love it.

"Temptation, if I try to fit in that goddamn thing, my feet are going to power through the floorboard. I'll be able to Flintstone us to New Mexico." He points at the car accusingly. "They didn't make it for a motherfucker my size."

"Well, they didn't make your truck for a woman my size," I say. "If I try to drive it, we aren't even going to make it out of the parking lot before I wreck."

"Wreck my truck and I'll be spanking your pretty little ass."

"How do you expect me to drive it when I can't even reach the peddles or see over the dashboard, Atlas?" I huff at him, annoyed. "I'm not built like freaking Goliath over here." I'm not even sure I'm capable of getting into his truck. I don't think it's lifted, but it's huge.

He glances at me and then at the truck and then back to me. "Fucking hell."

"The driver makes the rules."

"Yeah? You think so?"

"It's the law," I say primly. We both know I'm full of it, but his smile is awful arrogant. And hot. Lord, whichever angel crafted this man deserves a high five and a raise.

"Mmhmm," he says. "Get in the truck, Temptation. We're going to my place."

"What? Why?" I ask, suddenly wary.

"Because you can't drive my truck and I can't fit in that piss-poor excuse for a car. We're going with Option C."

"What's Option C?"

"You'll see."

"Why does that sound so ominous?"

"Because you have trust issues. Get your pretty ass in the truck."

CHAPTER SEVEN

Atlas

"Would you stop side-seat driving and leave me alone?" Gabbi says, grinning cheerfully as she zips in and out of traffic like a crazy person in my Challenger Hellcat. "You should be sleeping anyway."

"Not with you driving," I mutter. Either she's been fucking with me intentionally all day, or she really does treat the road like her own personal racetrack when she's behind the wheel. I have a feeling the answer is a little of both. She's far too comfortable driving like a maniac...which she's been doing since we left Silver Spoon Falls hours ago.

"You're speeding again."

"I'm going 70!"

"The speed limit is 65."

She shoots me a death glare. "You are the worst passenger ever, just in case no one ever told you. Next time, we're taking my car so you can't complain."

"There won't be a next time, Temptation. My new goal in life is to never need you to drive me anywhere ever again," I say wryly. "Matter of fact, my new goal in life is to make sure you never drive anywhere ever again, period. How many accidents have you been in?"

"None."

"Liar."

"Fine. One."

"Try again."

"Three, but one was only half my fault."

"How is half of an accident your fault?" I ask, truly mystified how that's possible. I unzip my bag while waiting for her to answer and grab a neck pillow. If she's going to kill me, I might as well be comfortable when I die. "That's like saying half a murder is your fault."

"I mean, maybe it is." She shrugs. "How should I know? I've never murdered anyone. Would you like to let me test your theory on you?"

She's definitely fucking with me now.

This is going to be a helluva long drive if she keeps being this goddamn cute and feisty. Erections aren't supposed to last longer than four hours. This is day three. At this point, fucking her is necessary for the survival of my cock.

"Explain, Temptation."

"A car was trying to merge in traffic and side-swiped me. I freaked out a little bit and swerved into another car. So see? Only half of that one is my fault."

"I'm not even going to ask about the other two," I mutter.

"I ran over an old lady and then took out a storefront."

I can't tell if she's joking or not. She sounds serious. And then she laughs, letting me know she's fucking with me again.

"You look like you're thinking about jumping out right now."

"Considered it," I admit. "But if you freaked out and swerved into another car, I'm guessing having me launch my big ass out of this car would end in a catastrophe. I happen to like my car with all the pieces attached."

"It is a nice car." She strokes the steering wheel like it's a damn cat.

Huh. My girl has a thing for cars. As soon as she saw this one, she fell in love. That makes two of us. With the car and with her. I'm guessing she's not ready to hear that last part though, so I keep it to myself for now. I will be fucking her on the hood as soon as humanly possible, though. It's moved to the top of my fuck-it list. I didn't even have one of those until I met her, now there are about eighty different ways and places I want to fuck her on it. "It is a nice car. Let's keep it that way."

"Fine. I suppose I'll stop torturing you now." She slows ever so slightly and flips the blinker on to get in the right lane. "Happy now, Spoilsport?"

"Thrilled," I say, deadpan.

She sticks her tongue out at me like a toddler.

"What did Jordan have to say?" I ask a few minutes later, watching her out of the corner of my eye.

"That he's going to kill you and leave pieces of your body all over the southwest if you lay a hand on me." She rolls her eyes. "And then he lectured me for half an hour on why I shouldn't be dating. And then we got into an argument."

"About me?"

"Yes? No? Sort of?" She shrugs like she isn't really sure which it is. "He's being completely unreasonable, as if he didn't just have sex with my best friend in Rome's BDSM club. He is so not the moral police right now."

"Hold up. Roman owns a BDSM club?" I turn to gape at her. "There's a BDSM club in Silver Spoon Falls?"

"Crap." She makes a face. "Pretend you didn't hear that."

"Oh, I definitely heard that."

"I'm serious, Atlas. You heard nothing."

I narrow my eyes on her. "Have you ever been to this club?"

"Oh, yes. Dozens of times."

A warning growl rumbles in my throat. "You better be fucking with me, Temptation."

"What if I'm not?" she asks, turning to glance at me in genuine curiosity.

"If you're asking if I'd judge you for it, the answer is no. You're allowed to be curious and have kinks. Shit, I plan to be curious and kinky as hell when I finally get you naked. But I've discovered that I'm a possessive, jealous mother-fucker when it comes to you, Temptation. The thought of other men even looking at you makes me want to break shit." I admit honestly. "I may damn well burn the club to the ground if you've been playing around inside."

"I haven't," she says quickly. "I was just teasing you. And I'm not just saying that to spare Rome's club. He and Jordan wouldn't let me through the doors even if I wanted to go—which I've never wanted to do."

"But you're curious."

She shrugs, her cheeks turning pink. "Maybe."

"You want to know what it's like to be fucked in public?"

"I...I don't know." Her tongue darts out, wetting her bottom lip. "I don't know what I like. You aren't the only virgin in the car, Atlas."

"Fuck," I groan, my hand moving to my dick as my balls throb. I grip myself through my sweats, squeezing to relieve a little pressure. "You want to explore? I'll let you live out every fantasy you have, baby. But no one else touches you. No one even sees you. I won't share you."

"I won't share either." She glances over at me again, her chocolate eyes darkening when she sees my hand on my dick. "Oh my gosh. Are you...?"

"Trying like hell to keep from demanding you tell me every filthy fantasy you have while I fuck my hand," I growl, squeezing tighter. "Christ. It hurts."

"S-show me," she whispers, her eyes darting to the road and then back to me.

I should tell her no and let her drive. That's the safe, sane thing to do. But she's a sweet little temptation, offering me a glimpse of heaven. How am I supposed to resist?

She whimpers when I jerk the band of my sweats down just enough for her to catch a glimpse of the head of my cock. Her gaze settles on it, her tongue between her lips.

"Once I finish, I'm getting you off while you focus on the road."

A shaky breath escapes her lips. She shivers next to me. I don't have to check her panties to know they're a soaked mess. If she were in a dress, I'd make her remove them and wrap them around my cock while I jerk off. Unfortunately for me, that's not in the cards at the moment.

So I settle for spitting in my hand and then grasping my cock, pulling the hard bastard free of my sweats.

"Tell me what you want me to do to you, Temptation."

"I..." She flounders, her eyes drifting back to the road. For a minute, I think she's going to clam up on me, but she doesn't. Her gaze flits back to me, full of determination.

Fuck. She's a fearless little thing. "Everything, Atlas. I want you to do everything to me."

"Goddamn," I growl, working my fist up and down my dick. I twist my wrist at the head. Pleasure dances from every nerve ending, throbbing in my balls. "When we get to the hotel tonight, I'm eating you for dinner, Temptation."

"Yes." She grips the steering wheel tightly, as if she's trying to keep herself together.

"And then I'm going to find out exactly how sweet you sound crying out my name while you're riding my cock." I work my hand up and down my shaft, trying to get myself there before some poor, unsuspecting trucker gets an eyeful. "Are you on birth control?"

"N-no."

"Good. Then there won't be anything stopping me from planting my kid in you."

"Atlas."

"It's too late for that, baby. It was too late the minute I saw you at the arena. I don't give a fuck about your brother. He won't stop me from claiming what belongs to me." Christ, just the thought of her carrying my kid has me ready to cum all over myself. But not yet. "Slip your hand inside your pants, Temptation. Let's see how good you look when you're touching yourself."

"T-that's not safe."

"Then find somewhere to pull over."

She bites her bottom lip and then nods. I expect her to pull to the side of the road, but she keeps driving for several minutes before taking an exit that seemingly leads nowhere. She rolls to a stop at the sign, looks both ways down the deserted road while the GPS tries to recalculate a course, and then turns right.

A couple of minutes later, she pulls off onto a gravel lane leading up a steep include into the trees. We bump along for several hundred yards before she finally stops. As soon as she has the car in park, I'm practically dragging her across the compact console onto my lap.

She lands with a groan, her legs spread to accommodate my size.

"Get your hand down your pants, Temptation," I order, biting her bottom lip. "I'm going to snap if you aren't coming for me in the next two minutes."

She jumps to obey, too turned on to hesitate. One perfectly manicured hand slips into the waistband of her leggings. She throws her head back, crying out as pure bliss overtakes her expression.

"Did you just fucking come?" I growl.

"Yes."

Jesus.

I drag her up several inches, giving me room to pull her leggings down. Her hand is still at work in her panties, which are fucking soaked with her juices. I growl, tugging them aside so I can see what she's doing.

Precum spills from the head of my cock at the sight of her. God, she's a horny little thing. Her fingers roll over her clit, coated with her sticky juices. She's bare and pink, glistening like the Holy Grail. Even though she's trembling, she doesn't stop what she's doing. She keeps going, moving her fingers over her clit, chasing another high.

"Again," I bark, one hand already around my dick. "I want to see it this time, Temptation."

"Working on it, Big Guy," she gasps and then mewls. "If we get caught, I'm blaming you."

"If we get caught, you're going to finish regardless of who's watching."

Heat flares even brighter in her eyes, turning them dark and glossy. Her fingers practically fly across her swollen clit, my threat doing exactly as intended. She likes the thought of being caught, of being watched. There's no way I'm willing to share even that much of her. But she doesn't have to know that right now. All she has to do is let her dirty little imagination run wild.

"Think they'll interrupt once they see you coming all over your pretty little fingers, Temptation? Or will they stand by quietly and watch the show?" I ask, jerking my cock roughly.

"Atlas," she whines.

"I think they'll beg to watch you finish, Temptation. Look how goddamn good you look right now. Jesus." I squeeze my cock as more precum wells from the slit. "It's taking everything I have to keep my hands to myself."

"W-who said you had to?"

Ah, hell.

I yank her forward on my lap until her knees are jammed into the seat behind me, and the heat of her pussy kisses the head of my cock. We both moan when we feel it. I bury my face in her throat, cursing up a blue streak.

"Come before I take this too far, Gabbi," I growl against her ear...not above begging if that's what it takes to get her there before I snap. She's sticky sweet, and burning hot. My cock is screaming for relief, and my hand is suddenly a piss-poor substitute for the heaven she's offering me.

Her first time won't be a quickie in the passenger seat. She deserves more than that.

"Help me," she pleads quietly. "T-touch me, Atlas."

"You're killing me, baby."

"I'm sorry!"

"Don't be. I fucking love it." I nip her throat and slip my hand between us, using it to grind the head of my cock against her clit. Her nails dig into my shoulder blades, a gasp of ecstasy echoing around the car.

She works her hips for me, helping to grind herself against my cock. Within seconds, I'm on the verge of coming all over her. I grit my teeth, fighting it off for as long as possible as she begins to tremble in my arms.

"That's it, Temptation," I breathe in her ear. "Come all over your man."

Her sweet voice rings out in a sultry aria as she tenses in my arms and then collapses forward, shivering and shaking. Arousal soaks the head of my cock, dripping all the way down my shaft.

I bury my face in her hair, groaning as I follow her over the edge into sweet oblivion. I make a mess of both of us, and I don't even give a shit about it. Because she's whispering my name like a prayer, and I've never felt more like a god than I do in this moment.

"You still with me?" I murmur, brushing her hair back from her face a few minutes later.

"Yes," she whispers.

I smile, an entire fucking section of my heart falling into her hands at the way she says it, all shy and sweet and adorable, like she's not sure how to react now that we're not caught in the moment.

"If this is my reward for getting nailed in the head with a puck, my brain is in serious trouble, Temptation."

"What? Why?"

"Because I'd absolutely take another puck to the head for five more minutes with you in my arms.

"How about we skip the puck next time?" she suggests, a smile in her voice. "You may have a big head, but your brain didn't grow to compensate. You probably shouldn't damage any more of it."

"I'll show you a big head," I growl, nipping her ear.

"I thought you just did," she sasses back.

"He is impressive, isn't he?"

"Meh," she says as if she's completely unimpressed.

I growl and tip her backward against the dash to kiss the fire from her mouth. Her laughter turns to a soft sigh of surrender. We make out until she grabs my hair a little too hard and my head throbs.

"I'm sorry!" She jerks back, holding her hands up like she just got caught with her hand in the cookie jar. "I didn't mean to hurt you."

"It's all good, baby." I rub the back of my head. The knot has gone down, but it still hurts like a motherfucker. "You didn't hurt me. It's just a little tender."

"Do you still have a headache?" Her expression is soft and full of worry.

"Not enough to worry about." I press my lips to her forehead. "Let's get cleaned up and get back on the road. You can play nurse when we get to the hotel."

"Only if you agree to get some sleep." She runs a fingertip beneath my right eye. "You look tired."

"I didn't sleep much. This gorgeous brunette with a smart-ass mouth kept my dick hard all night."

"Huh. Don't know her."

I chuckle, shaking my head as she shoots me a cheeky grin.

I find napkins in the console and use them to clean us up. She squirms on my lap, her face bright red as I wipe between her legs. But I made the mess, it's mine to clean up.

Once she's back in the driver's seat, her belt latched around her, she frowns at the navigation screen. "It wants us to keep going instead of turning around."

"It's probably rerouting us instead of having us backtrack."

"Through the mountains?"

"It knows more about the ways to get where we're going than I do, Temptation."

"Should I follow it?" She peers out of the windshield like she's trying to see into the future. "It doesn't look like it adds any extra time to the drive."

"Up to you," I say with a shrug. "You said you make the rules, remember?"

She sticks her tongue out at me and then mumbles under her breath. I'm not sure if she's insulting me, technology, or both. I lean back in the seat as she pulls off, following the GPS along the gravel path.

I check my phone and see a message from an unknown number. Judging by the message—a warning to keep my damn hands to myself or lose them—I assume it's Jordan.

I add his number to my contacts before texting him back.

Me: New phone. Who dis?

Cranky Future Brother-in-Law: You know who this is, fucker. Keep your hands off my sister.

Me: It's odd. I feel like someone told me the same thing recently, but I can't remember who.

Me: Or when.

Me: Or what.

Me: Oh well. It must not have been important.

I can't help but needle him. He tried to warn me away from Gabbi, and he threatened to send her to a convent. He deserves to sweat a little for that bullshit. I get that he's been responsible for her since she was a little girl. He probably feels more like a father to her than her brother. But I'm not the enemy here.

The sooner he learns we're on the same page when it comes to her, the better all our lives will be. She's worth fighting for, and I'll go down swinging if that's what it takes.

Cranky Future Brother-in-Law: I'm not fucking around, Jacks.

Me: You said you want me to marry your sister, right? Don't worry. I'm all over it.

Cranky Future Brother-in-Law: Tell her to answer her phone.

Her phone didn't even ring. I'm guessing she silenced it because she doesn't want to talk to him. I'm Team Gabbi on this one. At least for now. I'll convince her to call him after he has time to stew for a little while.

Me: Can't. She's driving. Safety first. Besides, I think she's giving you the silent treatment.

Cranky Future Brother-in-Law: I know. It's pissing me off.

Me: Maybe don't threaten to send her to a convent next time?

> Cranky: She started it.

> Me: Are you two?

> Cranky: You do remember that I own the Falcons, right? That basically means I own your sorry ass. Don't insult me. You may accidentally get loaned out to another team. I hear the East Coast is nice this time of year.

> Me: Liar. It's colder than a well digger's ass over there.

> Cranky: Take care of her, Jacks. I fucking mean it.

> Me: With my life.

It's not an empty promise. I mean that shit. He may be pissed, but he didn't lock her in a closet. He didn't try to stop her from coming with me. I figure that means something. He's trusting me with her, giving me a chance to prove that I'm a man worthy of her.

I plan to deserve every ounce of that trust.

I drop my phone into the console and reach for Gabbi. She glances over at me, smiling as I pull her hand toward my mouth to brush a kiss across her knuckles. Her smile only grows.

Fuck, I can't wait to see that expression on her face every day forever.

I lay our linked hands on the console and close my eyes. Despite what I told her, my head is still pounding. Every fucking time I breathe, a hot poker stabs me through the skull.

Fun times.

CHAPTER EIGHT

Gabbi

For a man named Atlas, he has a terrible navigation system. It doesn't reroute us back to the interstate. As he sleeps beside me, snoring and mumbling something about a puck wearing a sombrero, I drive deeper into the woods and mountains, swerving around and bouncing over potholes.

At some point, the woods become a certified forest, the canopy overhead thick enough to choke out what remains of the daylight. Lingering rays pierce through the dense canopy in places, causing little motes of dust to dance in midair. Those few sparkling rays give the scene an idyllic, almost dream-like quality. It's quiet underneath, almost peaceful.

I don't mind the detour much. It gives me plenty of time to think. When Jordan called me early this morning, trying to boss me into backing out of this trip, I refused. For the first time in a long time—perhaps for the first time ever—I did what I wanted to do, not what was expected of me. And it felt good.

He threatened to ship Atlas off to another team. I think I shocked us both when I threatened to follow him to wherever he went. Until that moment, the thought hadn't even entered my mind. Silver Spoon Falls is my home. I don't want to leave here. But for the first time, I think I'm realizing that home isn't a place, it's the people in it.

Since meeting him, Atlas has become one of the people who makes Silver Spoon Falls feel like home to me. He feels like home to me. I don't know what that means for me. I don't know what it means for us. But I want to be the kind of person brave enough to find out. Rome and Jordan are where they are in life because they took big risks.

It's my turn to take one too.

Jordan doesn't have to like it. He can stomp around and threaten to ship me off to convents or threaten to send Atlas to another team all he wants, but I'm not a little girl any longer. If I want something different in my life, I can't stand idly by and wait for someone else to make it happen. I've done that for far too long, letting Rome and Jordan call the shots.

I guess I thought I owed it to them, especially to Jordan. But love is unconditional. Family is forever. Those things aren't contingent upon whether or not I toe the line. Jordan may be worried about me, but I know deep down, that's not the life he'd want for me, either. He's just stubborn and overprotective and unwilling to admit that maybe I don't need him hovering over me anymore.

I think if he admits that I'm grown up, he has to face the fact that Hollie is too. And that's what really scares him. He's in love with my best friend, and he has no clue what to do about it. She was only eighteen when they met. In his eyes, she was just a kid, too young for him. So long as he can continue to convince himself that I'm too young to date, he doesn't have to deal with the fact that she's the same age I am.

I don't envy him. He's one of the most honorable people I know. Grappling with the fact that he's in love with someone so much younger than him is messing with his head. But that's their problem to solve, not mine. And I can't carry that cross for them.

I roll to a stop at a fork in the road, shifting my gaze from the road to the GPS. Dismay courses through me when, instead of directions, all I get is a spinning wheel that says rerouting. My gaze drifts to the corner of the screen, only to see a line slashed through the car's connectivity icon.

We no longer have signal.

I chew on my bottom lip, unsure which way to go. Neither road offers any clues. One looks just as good as the other, which is to say they're both pitted gravel lanes exactly like every other pitted lane I've been on for the last couple of hours.

But we've been going south and west for most of the ride, so I turn the car in that direction and set out. Every few minutes, my gaze drifts back to the navigation screen to see if we've gotten signal back, but it remains completely blocked out.

The sun sinks into its cradle, the last few rays dwindling quickly. The road gradually shifts from cement to gravel, the potholes growing larger. Trees press in closer as the gas gauge slips below a quarter of a tank, branches hanging over the road like spindly little arms reaching down from the inky blackness overhead.

"Please don't scratch his car," I whisper as if they're really listening. Out here, maybe they are. We're certainly far enough from civilization for magic to happen. Or to be eaten by a chupacabra.

The car descends into a pothole, the bottom scraping.

I grit my teeth, slowing to a crawl as I inch forward, trying not to damage anything as I work our way through it. When we get back to something resembling civilization, I'm writing a sternly worded letter to the GPS people.

Except...halfway through the pothole, I push the gas and the tires just spin. The car won't move. I give it more gas, sending up a prayer that I didn't just get us stuck in the middle of nowhere.

The engine purrs. The tires spin. We don't go anywhere.

"Crap."

Naturally, Atlas decides now is the perfect time to jolt awake. He sits up, scrubbing his hand down his face. "Where the fuck are we?"

"Um, in the forest?"

I feel more than see him turn toward me.

"Please don't freak out," I say, fumbling to find the overhead light. "But I think we might be stuck."

"Stuck?"

"Yes, stuck." I press the gas to emphasize the point.

He listens to the engine purr and the tires spin without us going anywhere.

"Fuck," he mumbles. "Can you reach the flashlight tucked right under the lip of your seat, Temptation?"

I put the car in park and unlatch my seatbelt to feel for the light. My hand closes around it and I fumble it out, passing it over to him. "Be careful. We're in a pothole."

He nods and carefully steps out, losing a good foot of height when he does.

Good grief. Maybe I drove us into a crater instead of a pothole.

"Stay in the car, Temptation. It's muddy."

The knot in my stomach grows five sizes.

"Okay," I whisper.

He carefully makes his way around the car, assessing the situation, before he comes back to me. "If we can get traction under the back tires, you should be able to drive out. They're stuck in a mudhole inside the pothole."

"Okay."

"Can you pop the trunk for me? I should have some litter in there we can use."

I fish around for the trunk release before he directs me to it. He rummages around for a few minutes before I lose track of him in the darkness. I peer all around, keeping an eye on the forest around us. It no longer seems idyllic and peaceful, but ominous and threatening, as if a thousand hidden dangers lurk in the tree line, watching us.

I pull my phone out again, checking for signal. Instead of bars indicating the strength of my signal to the nearest tower, my phone simply says No Service. How there are still places with roads and no service, I don't know. Yet here we are. Lost in the middle of nowhere because I took a risk.

Atlas pops up beside my door. I jump, startled, and drop my phone.

"Sorry, Temptation." He pulls the door open, his expression contrite. "Didn't mean to scare you. I've got the litter down and wedged two sturdy branches under the tires to help us get traction. Think you can drive it out of here?"

"I think so."

"Give it a shot then, baby. I'll wait until you're out in case I need to help push it along."

"Atlas, you can't push the car. You have a concussion!"

"Don't plan to push it with my head, Temptation." He smirks at me. "But I'm a helluva lot bigger than you are. If it needs a little boost, I'll be able to move it along a lot better than you will."

I try to find a flaw in his logic, but there isn't one. The only thing I'm going to push if I try is myself right into the mudhole. Strength training days at the gym are my least favorite days...which is precisely why I end up skipping most of them.

"Fine, but please be careful."

"You worried about me?"

"Yes. You aren't allowed to die in the woods. I forbid it."

He reaches out, brushing his thumb along my bottom lip. "I'm not going to die in the woods. If I did, you'd be on your own. You think I'm going to get out of the way for some other motherfucker to make a move? Hell no."

Of course, that's what he's concerned about.

"Go push the car, Atlas."

He chuckles and backs away from my door.

I take a breath, send up a prayer, and work with him to get us unstuck. Half an hour later, it's apparent that the car isn't going anywhere without a tow truck and Jesus.

Atlas reaches the same conclusion a few moments later. He gives up trying to He-Man it from the mud and starts around the side of the car toward my door. He's covered in mud and swearing. He's also stumbling slightly.

"There's no way out of that fucking pothole."

"We could call for help. Do you have signal? I don't."

He's shaking his head before I even finish talking. "Tried it already. I don't have a single bar. Tried to call Coach while I was rummaging through the trunk, but it wouldn't even try to connect."

My face falls.

"Hey." He tugs me into his arms. "We're okay, Temptation. I'll just hike until I reach civilization. We're in the middle of Texas. Civilization can't be that fucking far away."

"That's a bad idea. We're already lost. The last thing we need to do is split up and one of us get even more lost. Besides, I'm not staying in this car by myself."

"It's not safe out here, Temptation."

"Exactly!" I cry. "That's exactly why you shouldn't be out trooping through the woods alone. Either we both go or neither of us goes."

"We're not staying out here tonight, Gabbi. Fuck that. It's already cold and will only get colder. We've got a fourth of a tank. It's not going to last until morning. Not to mention, there are all kinds of wild animals in these woods. I'm not going to risk your safety."

"It would be at risk if we stayed in the car," I argue.

"We'll walk until we find something," he says, his voice firm.

I open my mouth to argue, but he silences me with a hard kiss. "I'm not risking you freezing to death by sleeping in the car, Gabbi. Forget it."

"Fine," I huff. "But if we get more lost or get eaten by a tiger, it's your fault."

"Tigers don't live in the woods."

"I know!" I cry. "But every other terrifying thing does, so they might as well join the party."

He chuckles quietly, pulling me from the car. "Come on, baby. Let's get our gear and go find help."

Forty-five minutes later, I'm ready to crawl out of my skin. We haven't come across a single other person or vehicle. Every little sound in the woods freaks me out. I feel like we're being hunted, and I'm ready to cry.

I had one job, and I failed epically. Now, Atlas is stuck in the woods with a concussion, and no one knows where we are. *We* don't even know where we are. If we get too lost, it could be days before anyone finds his car and starts looking for us.

It's not a good position to be in.

"Hold up, baby," he says suddenly, shining his flashlight into the woods.

"What? Why?" I grab his arm, my heart leaping into my throat.

"I think there's a cabin back there."

Excitement shoots through me.

Atlas strolls closer to the side of the road, sweeping his flashlight along the tree line. I notice the partially obscured driveway the same moment he does. It looks like it hasn't been used in a while, but it's definitely there.

We head toward it at the same time. He keeps his flashlight trained on the woods, scanning for a glimpse of whatever he thought he saw. The light hits nothing but trees until we're right up on the driveway and then the dark outline of view. It's set back from the roadway, tucked neatly between two massive oak trees.

There are no lights on or other signs of life. But it's the first sign of civilization I've seen in over two hours. That has to be a good thing...right?

"It doesn't look like anyone lives here."

"They don't," he says. "I'm guessing we're somewhere in the Guadalupe Mountains. A cabin out this far is either a rental cabin or a ranger cabin. Either way, it's good news for us."

"How is an empty cabin good news for us?"

"If it's a ranger cabin, they'll have a way to call out. If it's one of their rentals, it's a place to hunker down," he says. "I don't know about you, but I'd really like to get the fuck out of the woods for a while."

"Me too."

"Then let's go check it out."

I hesitate for a moment, eyeing the cabin. It looks like a murder cabin to me. But unless the ghost of Satan haunts the place, I think I'd rather take my chances inside. At least there aren't chupacabras inside.

I slowly climb the overgrown driveway, praying nothing jumps out of the woods at us. Thankfully, the closer we get, the less murdery the cabin looks. It's old, but it's not falling apart. There are even blinds over the windows. That has to be a good sign, right?

Murderers probably don't use miniblinds. At least not way out here.

"I'll go check it out. You wait on the porch," Atlas says.

"No way." Call me crazy, but getting dragged out into the woods and axe murdered while he's inside does not sound like a good time to me. That's how murder-in-the-woods movies always start. More or less. "I'm going in with you."

"It's safer out here."

"Oh, really? Because I've seen a lot of horror movies, and the person who stays behind is always the first to die.

I'm trying to be Final Girl material here, Big Guy. I'm not getting eaten by a chupacabra while you're inside."

His lips twitch. "A chupacabra?"

"Feels like chupacabra woods to me," I mumble, shoving my hands deeper into my pockets. It's already getting chilly out. Much longer, and it'll be downright frigid.

"How is it possible that you get us lost in the woods and you're still the cutest fucking thing I've ever seen?"

"Technically, your car got us lost in the woods. I tried to tell you it was on some BS, but you trusted the car. You convinced me to trust the car." I shoot him a look that silently judges him. "It's your fault, really."

"Get inside before we give your chupacabra a show, Temptation."

I reluctantly scurry toward the cabin as every living animal in the woods glares at me. At least, that's what it feels like. I think he feels the same thing because he wastes no time getting us to the front door. The porch is soft beneath our feet and wobbles dangerously, but we silently agree to risk it anyway.

I think my hockey hunk may be just a little bit afraid of nature.

Something howls in the distance, and I quickly decide that makes two of us.

CHAPTER NINE

Atlas

"I'm sorry I got us lost in the woods. And then got us stuck in a crater. And then got us more lost in the woods," Gabbi says, wringing her hands as she paces around the cabin. It doesn't take long for her to make a pass from one side to the other. The place isn't that big.

The cabin is a solitary room consisting of a bed with an old iron frame and headboard, a table and a single wooden chair, and a plaque on the wall declaring the place a historic landmark. There is no electricity. The only source of heat is the fireplace across from the bed. It's the only source of light, too.

Surprisingly, there is water in the closet-sized bathroom...which consists entirely of an old sink and a toilet. It's rustic as hell, but it's infinitely better than the car. It's infinitely safer too. We're not stuck in a pothole in the middle of the road with a limited supply of gas in here.

I'm less concerned with being stranded, and more concerned with Gabbi. She's anxious and antsy, unable to sit still. She keeps apologizing for getting us stranded as if it's her fault GPS decided to reroute us. The best I can figure, it's trying to take us from Highway 69 to 258 and chose to route through the national park to do it.

"It's all good, baby. We'll get out of here in the morning and be back on the road." I continue pulling shit out of my bag, one eye on her.

She makes another circuit and then spins to face me, her mouth open to say something. Whatever it was, she doesn't say it. Her gaze lands on the snacks piled on the table and go comically wide.

"Holy crap, Atlas. Did you pack actual clothes in your bag or just snacks?"

"Mostly snacks." I shrug, unrepentant about packing like a five-year-old.

"Do they not feed you?" she asks, eyes still wide.

"My teammates never bring their own shit," I complain. "They're like the neighbor who wants to borrow sugar to make cereal, only they show up with nothing to put the sugar in. So you give them a bowl. And then they need to borrow milk. Once they've got that, they need cereal, and a spoon. In short, if you give a hockey player a snack, he's going to want the whole goddamn fridge because his ass packed nothing useful."

Gabbi's lips twitch as she fights a smile. "So you pack your entire pantry instead of clothes?"

"Feeding the fuckers is easier than listening to them complain the entire trip, so I started coming prepared." I shrug again, holding out a hand toward her. "You're welcome, by the way. My snack hoarding means you aren't going to have to eat that single can of hot dog chili we found in the cabinet."

She grimaces at the thought of the hot dog chili. It looks like it's been in the cabinet over the table for a good fifteen years. Maybe longer. She sashays toward me to slip her hand into mine.

I reel her in, not stopping until she has no choice but to climb onto the bed with me. She settles beside me, her shoulder pressed to mine as she surveys the snacks.

"Are those Scooby Doo fruit snacks?"

"Is there any other kind of fruit snack?" I quirk a brow, picking up the package in question. "These things are fucking delicious."

She beams at me, her expression soft in the flickering firelight. "You're a man of many mysteries, Atlas Jacks."

"Nothing mysterious about me, Temptation. I like hockey, food, and you." I think about it before adding, "In reverse order."

"I'm at the top of the list, huh?" She bats her lashes at me, clearly up to something. "What does that earn me, Big Guy?"

"Anything you want." I hide the fruit snacks behind my back. "Except my fruit snacks."

Her face falls into an adorable pout. "But they're the best kind."

"I know. Why do you think I'm not sharing?"

She growls, snapping her teeth at me playfully as she lunges as if to forcibly steal my fruit snacks. I pluck her up from the bed mid lunge, toppling her over backward. We land in a sea of protein bars, Twizzlers, and individual sized Pringles.

She laughs up at me, her eyes bright enough to light up the entire fucking cabin. I forget about feeding her. I forget about where we are. I forget everything but how beautiful she is and how badly I need to kiss her.

My lips brush hers, earning a soft sigh from her lips. She melts beneath me, her arms coming up to wrap around my neck. I drink from her lips, perfectly willing to gorge myself on her. Fuck fruit snacks. She's my guilty pleasure, my secret addiction, and the one thing I won't share.

"You're so goddamn beautiful," I murmur, brushing strands of hair back from her face. It's not hard to see why Jordan is so protective over her. Five minutes with her makes it obvious she's priceless. Her brother knows how motherfuckers think. We see something like her—something so pure—and want it for ourselves.

"So are you." She smiles up at me, her expression honest and open and so fucking sweet I have to kiss her again.

"Are you falling in love with me yet, Temptation?" I whisper, brushing my nose against hers. I'm already there with her. I didn't even fall. I think I took a swan dive, jumping headfirst into it. It's impossible not to love her.

I'm not sure I even expect her to answer, the question just spills from my lips. But she answers anyway, as honest as ever. "I'm falling so hard," she admits. "And so fast."

"Good," I whisper, her words sending a powerful wave through me. It's triumph and something deeper...adoration, devotion. I'm not sure I know the name for it, But I know there's not a single other person on the planet I'd rather be lost in the woods with. There isn't a single other person who could claim even a piece of my heart. The whole thing belongs to her.

"Kiss me," she demands, turning her face up to mine.

I take the liberty she gives me, brushing featherlight kisses all over her face before I arrive back at her lips. I hover there for a moment, earning a frustrated whine from her. She doesn't like to be denied.

I file that away for later, sinking into her kiss like she's my favorite dessert. Shit, I think she may be my favorite flavor, period. She's sweet like vanilla, spicy like cinnamon. It's an intoxicating combination, one that's somehow uniquely her.

Her arms tighten around my neck, drawing me closer. I crawl over her, nudging her legs apart to fit myself between them, needing to touch her in as many places as possible, to feel her in as many ways as possible.

She moans beneath me, arching from the bed to seam our bodies together. More electric shocks flow through me, hardening my cock. The pounding in my head all but vanishes, pain unable to survive where pleasure rules.

I grind against her, run my hands all over her, trying to memorize the feel of her beneath me, to imprint it into my brain so the memory becomes an indelible part of me.

She pants beneath me, her legs around my waist as she tries to figure out a rhythm. Her hips roll as if she were born to fuck, born to please. Goddamn. I need inside her more than I need air.

I slip my hands beneath her shirt.

"Do you want me to stop?" I ask, pausing when she startles beneath me.

"Not if you value your life."

Well, I guess that's clear enough, isn't it?

Still....

"If we keep going, I'm going to be riding you bare tonight, Temptation. Once I have you, I won't give you up."

"Could you now?" Her doe eyes meet mine, full of curiosity.

"Fuck no," I rasp. "But I'm trying to be a gentleman and at least pretend you have a choice here." How far we go is always up to her. I won't push for more than she's ready to give. But she sealed her fate the instant she let me touch her in the car earlier today. Hell, maybe she sealed it the moment she agreed to come with me. I won't give her up now. Even if I have to spend the rest of my life convincing her that I'm worth the risk. Even if I have to push to get her where I want her.

If that makes me an asshole, I'll wear the title with pride. When it comes to her, I'll be the biggest asshole I need to be to tie her to me. I've spent my whole life training for a sport, pushing myself beyond the breaking point for a game. If anyone thinks I won't do the same for this sweet little Temptation, they're wrong. Because this time, it isn't a game. It's my whole future on the line here.

"Don't stop, Atlas," she says, commanding me now. Demanding that I give her what she wants. She's as caught by what's happening between us as I am, as incapable of denying or ignoring it. Thank fucking God.

I kiss her again, spilling my devotion into her, and breathing her desire into my lungs. We grind against each other, driving each other higher with our clothes still on. Until it's not enough for me anymore.

I slowly pull her shirt up her body, pulling away from her mouth to follow the path with my lips and tongue. She's soft and sweet everywhere, the perfect little morsel. Her skin turns to gooseflesh beneath my lips, her head falling back against the old mattress on a soft moan.

My lips close over her nipple through her bra, tonguing the hard bud, biting gently. Her little moans turn to louder cries. She's sensitive, reacting to every touch, every kiss. My dick throbs when I drag the cups of her bra down, exposing her breasts.

I knew they'd be perfect, but damn. Perfect looks even better than I imagined.

My teeth close around her left nipple. I bite down, flicking my tongue against it at the same time.

"Atlas!" she sobs, her voice full of wonder.

I do the same thing to her right nipple as I attack the clasp of her bra, trying to get it off her. It joins her shirt on the floor, leaving her topless beneath me. I can't resist pulling my dick out to squeeze the hard bastard as I stare down at her. She's a work of art.

She whimpers when she sees my dick in my hand, her eyes locked on the sight.

I pump my fist a few times, letting her watch. Her eyes grow darker. She squirms beneath me, restless and eager.

"Ah, goddamn," I groan, my head kicking back as her small hand wraps around my shaft above mine.

"Teach me," she whispers.

I do as commanded, releasing my dick to wrap my hand around hers. I show her how hard to hold me, how to pump her perfect hand to drive me crazy. I'm my own worst enemy in this moment, giving her the secrets to my demise.

She uses them against me, uses them to annihilate me. She learns quickly, leaving me gasping above her.

"Enough," I groan, pulling her hand away before she has me coming all over her again. When I come this time, it'll be inside her where I belong. But not yet. Not until I know exactly how she tastes.

She whines in protest, trying to fight me to keep her hand on my dick.

"Settle down before I turn your luscious ass red, Temptation."

My threat pulls a moan from her lips. Interesting. I file that away for later, fully intending to find out just how much she enjoys the feel of my hand against her ass. But not tonight. Not for her first time.

I kiss my way down her body, lavishing more attention on her. I couldn't stop myself if I wanted to do it. Every inch of her deserves my undivided attention. Every inch of her is delectable.

She isn't shy. She doesn't try to hide herself from me. It's as if she knows that there isn't a spot on her that isn't infinitely attractive to me. I love every dip, every curve, every adorable little roll. Each one makes my cock hard.

Each one is worthy of the highest praise. She was made to topple kingdoms and start wars.

"Lift up," I murmur, hooking my hands into the waistband of her pants.

She lifts her ass from the bed, allowing me to peel her leggings and panties down her body. I focus on the task at hand, trying like hell not to look at the little slice of heaven between her legs before she's naked.

Once I've got her stripped bare, I rise from the bed and quickly pull my clothes off. She watches with wide eyes.

"Keep looking at me like that and you'll have me thinking I'm something special, Temptation," I murmur, wrapping my fist around my cock as I crawl back onto the bed with her.

"You are," she says, her eyes locked on me. "I've never seen anything like you before, Atlas."

"Yeah?" I smile, feeling fifty feet tall and bullet proof with that look in her eyes. I know what I look like. I know what women say about me. Most may be leery of me, but they don't mind looking. I never gave a shit until this moment. Until her. Her opinion matters. I'll be the man she's waking up to for the rest of her life. She should enjoy it.

"You're beautiful."

"You think so? Then lay back, spread those legs, and show me how much you enjoy looking at me, Temptation."

Heat climbs into her cheeks as she lowers herself back down. She spreads her legs slowly, giving me another glimpse of heaven. She's soaked, her hard little clit peeking from between her bare lips.

I groan, my mouth watering at the sight. Fucking hell. I've never seen anything prettier than her spread out beneath me, all sweet and ripe and eager. I crawl between her legs, running my lips up her right leg.

Her heady scent hits my system and my fucking mouth waters.

Her thigh trembles beneath my lips as I pull her closer, lowering myself at the same time. Her pussy is at eye level, inches from my face. When I die, this is how I want to go. Between her legs, looking at my idea of heaven.

"Atlas!" she gasps, back bowing off the bed when I take my first lick of her. I'm not slow about it. Fuck that. I need her taste on my tongue more than I need my next breath. This isn't going to be nice and easy. I fully intend to have her addicted to my mouth and what it can do.

Her taste bursts on my tongue and rationality threatens to spiral away. I'm in so much fucking trouble here. Christ, she's the best thing I've ever eaten. I drag her closer to my mouth and set to work.

Her sweet cries fill the cabin as I lick and suck and feast on her. Her juices drip down my chin, covering me in her. She grinds against my face, babbling nonsense, clawing at the bed, moaning my name.

Fuck. I could stay like this forever.

I grind my dick against the mattress, working first one finger and then another into her. She's tight as hell, making me fight for it. I do, growling against her pussy as I fuck her with two fingers, trying to get her ready for me.

She's so fucking hot around them, I already know I won't last when it's my dick breaching that tight little hole. I'll be breeding her in seconds, minutes if I'm lucky. That's all right though. We've got all night, and my dick seems to have superpowers around her. I'll make it up to her on rounds two and three.

"Goddamn, Gabbi," I groan against her pussy. "You've got me so fucking hard it hurts, but it's the sweetest damn torture."

"Atlas."

"I can't wait to breed this little thing." I run my tongue around her clit again. "Think I can get you pregnant on the first try?"

"I...I..."

"You'll have to be a good girl and take all of me. But you can do it, can't you?" I pull one lip after the other into my mouth, licking them clean. "You're practically begging for it right now."

"Yes!"

"Then fucking come so I can get to work." I curl my fingers up, searching for her G-spot. I find it, rubbing firmly as I bat her clit with my tongue over and over.

She practically levitates off the bed, shouting my name as the orgasm slams into her hard and fast. Her pussy locks around my fingers, squeezing like a vise. Her juice floods my mouth, soaking my face.

I growl, grinding my dick against the mattress, fucking desperate to get inside her. But I don't stop what I'm doing. Not until she falls limp beneath me, adorable little puffs of sound escaping her lips.

I prowl over her, taking her mouth in a deep kiss, letting her taste how fucking good she is. She moans when she tastes herself on my lips, her legs locking around my waist.

"I can't wait any longer." I'm not sure I'll survive the next thirty seconds if I don't spend them inside her. Actually, that's not true. I know I won't survive them if I'm not inside her.

"Make love to me, Atlas. Make me yours."

"You're already mine." I nip her shoulder and then nuzzle her throat, notching my dick at her entrance. "You've been mine since the moment you walked into the arena."

"I think I was yours long before that," she whispers, staring up at me with those fathomless doe eyes. "I think I've always been yours."

Fuck yeah. There's a reason I never felt compelled to try to date, a reason no one ever caught my interest. They simply weren't her. I've just been waiting for fate to bring me to her. It did when her brother bought the majority stake in the new team. It did when it sent me to Silver

Spoon Falls. It did when it brought her to the arena to verbally kick my ass. It's been guiding me toward her every step of the way.

I claim her mouth in a deep kiss, pouring my gratitude into her. In three days, she's completely changed the trajectory of my life, knocking it into a brand new orbit. I fucking love everything about it.

I love her. How could I not when she's the most priceless thing in this world?

"Gabbi."

Her eyes flutter open, her attention focusing on me.

"I love you." I slowly push forward, holding her captive with my gaze. I see the minute my confession registers. See the joy and awe take root and grow. I see the same powerful emotion coursing through me reflected like stars in her eyes.

The head of my cock slips inside.

"Atlas," she moans.

I go slow, trying like hell not to hurt her. We kiss and touch and explore as I slip inside inch by exquisite, excruciating inch. If she feels any pain, it's fleeting. She tenses when her barrier tears, but she doesn't cry out. She doesn't even flinch.

I pause anyway, giving her a moment as my lips trail all across her face, raining kisses down on her. Once she's squirming beneath me, I push forward again, surging deep.

Her gasp of delight lets me know she's right there with me. I bury myself to the hilt in her and then pause again, reveling in the moment. In the feel of her wrapped around me. In the warmth of her embrace and the heat in her eyes. Even lost in the woods with a concussion, the moment is perfect. I wouldn't change a thing about it.

I fuck her slow at first, listening to the way her breath hitches and she gasps. Getting lost in the way her muscles clench around me every time I thrust deep. Fucking hell. I could spend a lifetime just like this.

She moves with me, rolling her hips, taking me all the way. All the filthy shit I said to her earlier is still there, waiting to burst free. But I whisper to her instead. Telling her how fucking incredible she feels. How goddamn beautiful she looks taking my cock. How crazy I am about her.

Those are the confessions this moment calls for. There will be plenty of time for the dirty talk later. I intend to do a lot of it. My girl is curious and eager to explore. She likes the dirty and the kinky. I'll give her enough of both to last a lifetime. But I'll give her this too. Moments not marked by the need to fuck and possess and dominate but tinged with the fierce devotion she's earned from me.

She mewls as her orgasm looms closer, her eyes glossy. I shift positions slightly, allowing me to go deeper. We get lost in the rhythm. Every time she gasps my name, my control slips, and I fuck her a little harder, a little deeper.

Until I'm pounding into her, my balls slapping against her sex with every thrust.

"Come for me, baby," I groan, slipping my hand between us to zero in on her clit. "Let me feel it all over my cock."

"Atlas." Her little gasp of delight threatens to send me careening over the edge. It's so innocent, so full of wonder. As if she didn't know it was possible to feel so much pleasure hitting her at once.

I rub her clit, pumping my hips as she trembles on the edge.

"Come, Temptation. Get yourself nice and ready for me to fill that womb," I growl against her ear. "The harder you come, the easier it'll be for me to plant my kid in you."

She clenches around me, crying out my name.

"I'm going to keep you on my cock tonight until you're good and pregnant." I nip her throat and then her collarbone. "You'll feel me dripping from this hot little hole every time you move tomorrow."

My balls are ready to explode, but she's fighting it. Fighting me. Not because she doesn't want it, but because she wants me to claim it. She can't help but demand I earn it. She's fucking perfect for me in every way.

Maybe there's room for a little dirty in this moment, after all.

I press my lips to her ear again, making sure she hears me. "You can't stop me, Temptation. I own this pussy now. So be a good girl and fucking come already." I drive into her hard and deep, grinding against her clit at the same time.

She falls like dominoes, shattering into pieces around me.

I roar her name as her cunt locks down around my dick, sending ripples of pleasure straight to my balls. They give up the fight, cum shooting up my shaft to spill into her in thick ropes. I pump my hips, driving into her again and again as the pleasure becomes unbearable.

Her sobs of ecstasy let me know she's right there with me, feeling every rapturous moment. I pour everything into her, giving her my soul.

CHAPTER TEN

Gabbi

Atlas keeps me up half the night, making love to me over and over. I'm not complaining. Every time is better than the last, which shouldn't be possible because they're all perfect. He makes love to me torturously slow, and then fucks me with his hand around my throat and his filthy words ringing in my ears.

By the time he collapses beside me, too exhausted to move, I'm permanently settled on a cloud of euphoria, unable to come down. I expect him to sleep hard. I know he has to be exhausted after trying to get the car unstuck, walking here, and then making love half the night.

But he tosses and turns all night as if he can't get comfortable. Every time I look at him, his eyes are still closed though. His brow is furrowed too, as if he feels pain even in his sleep.

I finally fall asleep, only to wake up a little after dawn when he starts moving around. He looks worse than he did yesterday morning. But there's a contentment in his eyes that wasn't there yesterday, as if he's perfectly at peace.

I can tell he's hurting though. I have to call his name three times to get his attention as we gorge ourselves on protein bars.

"Are you okay?" I ask, the first inklings of serious worry setting in. We pushed too hard last night. He should have been resting instead of making love to me.

"Fine," he says. "My goddamn neck is killing me, though. I think I slept wrong."

I don't think that's the problem at all. Neck pain is a common concussion symptom. It's also a worrisome one. He should be getting better and experiencing fewer symptoms. The fact that new ones are presenting instead means he may not be returning to the ice anytime soon, certainly not a week and a half from now.

"How's your head this morning?"

"Pounding like a jackhammer." He grimaces in distaste. "Next time I decide to get in front of Reid and a puck, please remind me that I'm an idiot."

"Miles."

"Huh?"

"Miles hit you with the puck."

"That's what I said."

"No, you said Reid."

"Miles, Reid. Same asshole, different package." He waves me off as if it doesn't matter and then holds out his hand to me. "We should probably get out of here and head back to the car. If we have to do much walking today, we should start sooner rather than later."

"Yeah," I agree, vowing to keep a close eye on him today. As soon as we're back to civilization, he's going to the doctor. I'll knock him out and drag him myself if I have to do it.

We dress quickly and then repack everything into our bags. I try to convince him to let me carry them, but he refuses, just like he did last night.

Within twenty minutes, we're ready to head out. I exit the cabin ahead of him, taking my first good look around. The woods march right up to the edge of the cabin, leaving very little cleared space around it. In the light of day, it looks less murdery than it did last night...but not nearly enough to convince me that it isn't haunted by the ghost of some crazed woodsman. Unfortunately, it looks far worse for wear too. I don't think it's been used regularly in a long time.

The porch is rotted, the wood giving way in places. One big section is soft under my feet. I hurry my steps in search of more solid ground.

"Be careful," I call back to Atlas. "The porch isn't holding up well."

"At least the cabin didn't fall down around us," he mutters as if that were a real possibility.

I step onto solid ground, breathing a sigh of relief. I didn't even consider the possibility that the structure could collapse. I'm kind of glad I didn't consider it. That would have kept me up all night.

An ominous groaning sound comes from behind me as I stretch my arms over my head. I whip around just in time to see Atlas crossing through the weakest area of the porch.

"You should hurr..."

One minute, he's walking across the porch. The next, the rotted wood gives way beneath his feet.

"Shit!" he curses, wobbling as an entire section of wood splinters apart beneath his feet. He jolts forward, trying to get out of there, but the porch isn't done collapsing. The plank where he intended to land cracks in half, the floor of the porch becoming little more than a gaping maw of splintered wood and rusty nails.

He plummets through the broken floorboards as others come loose around him. I cry out, stumbling forward, only to immediately jump back as the entire right side of the porch shudders and then collapses. It pulls away from the cabin with a loud roar of sound that sends chills racing up my spine.

I watch in horror as the wood topples, landing directly on top of Atlas.

It's over as quickly as it began. The loud echoes fade, leaving an eerie, terrifying silence in its wake. I hold my breath for a moment, terrified the cabin is going to come down, too. But it stands firm, whatever rot took the porch not having worked deeply enough through the entire cabin to topple it.

"Atlas!" I drop everything in my hands and race forward, flinging splintered boards aside in a frantic search. "Atlas!"

He doesn't answer me. He doesn't make a sound.

I sob his name, grabbing wood as fast as I can, trying to get him out. Rusty nails scrape my palms. Splinters gouge into my flesh. I don't care. He's under there, and he isn't answering me.

He's hurt.

Please, God, only let him be hurt. Don't let him be dead. Don't let him be dead. I repeat it like a mantra, tears dripping down my face, blood running down my hands from cuts.

"Atlas!" Oh, thank you Jesus. I can see him. He's at the edge of the collapsed structure, face down. I don't know if he's breathing, but he isn't moving. Another sob bursts from my lips, as I drop to my knees beside him, reaching for his hand.

I hold my breath, terror clogging my throat as I check for his pulse.

"Thank you. Oh, God, thank you," I sob, nearly collapsing when I find it. His heart is still beating. He isn't dead. I've never been so afraid in my life. "Atlas, wake up."

Despite shaking him, he doesn't move or make a sound. Relief turns to alarm and then another wave of panic rolls in. It's been at least five minutes since the porch collapsed. If he got knocked out, he should be waking up by now.

The fact that he isn't even moving is seriously concerning.

But I can't even assess him until he's out of harm's way. If the rest of the porch collapses, there's a good possibility it'll land right on top of him. He's still wedged beneath it, only a few feet of clear space above him.

I use clothes from my bag and a few pieces of wood to fashion a brace for his neck to keep him immobile while I'm moving him. There isn't a lot of space to work with, and I don't have time to make it perfect, but I do what I can and pray it's enough.

I grab his arm and slowly start dragging him out.

On a good day, he's a lot of man to move. On a day like today, when he's dead weight, he seems even bigger. And somehow so much more vulnerable at the same time.

I end up on my butt, with him partially draped across my lap so I can help stabilize his neck. I use my feet to propel us backward, ignoring the small rocks and weeds jabbing me. By the time I have him out of immediate danger, I'm sweating and crying, trying not to give into hysteria.

If I can't take care of the man I love when he's completely reliant on me to get him out of this alive, I have no business taking care of anyone. But he didn't even move through the entire ordeal, and that's not a good sign.

He's bruised and bloody, with a two-inch gash across the right side of his forehead. Another head injury. And this time, it's one that knocked him unconscious.

I quickly assess him, but he doesn't have any broke bones. No other obvious signs of trauma, either. He needs more aid than I can give him out here, though. I use the flashlight on my phone to check his pupils. They're slower to respond than I'd like. He needs a hospital and doctors. His brain could be swelling or bleeding.

"Please, don't leave me," I plead, gently touching his face. "Please, Atlas. I need you to be okay." I just found him. I haven't even told him that I love him. He said it last night, but I didn't say it back. I was too caught up in the moment. Now, the moment has passed and I'm terrified I'll never get the chance to tell him that he has my whole heart.

No. That's not going to happen. I'm going to get him out of here. No matter what it takes, he's not dying in the woods because I got us lost.

I set to work making a litter of sturdy branches woven together with the clothes from my bag. It's the most pitiful looking thing I've ever seen in my life. But it doesn't have to hold up for long. Just long enough for me to get him inside to safety so I can hike out for help.

We had reception a few miles before the road split. If I can make it back there, I can call out and get help to him. Maybe by now, someone has even found his car, and they're looking for us.

It takes an hour to drag him around to the back of the cabin. I carefully test the tiny back porch, going so far as to jump up and down to make sure it'll hold. It's not nearly as far off the ground as the front porch and it seems sturdy. I wrap my hand in a towel and break the glass out of the door so I can unlock it.

Once it's open, I start the process of hauling him up the steps. Every time he bounces, I cry an apology. I don't know if he can hear me, but I hope he can. I hope he knows I'm trying to save his life.

My legs feel like rubber by the time I get him inside. There's no way I'll be able to get him in the bed, so I don't try. I don't relight the fire either. If he does have brain swelling, the only thing I can do for him right now is hope he gets cold enough without the fire while I'm gone to keep it to a minimum.

"I'm coming back for you," I promise, using his facial recognition to unlock his phone to tap out a note to him in case he wakes up. Please, God, let him wake up.

I lay the phone on his chest, press a kiss to his scruffy jaw, and scurry out. By the time my feet hit the ground, I'm running. I race as fast as I can down the overgrown driveway and out onto the narrow trail.

In the light of day, it's easy to see what we couldn't last night. This isn't a road at all but a logging trail of some sort. One that clearly hasn't been used in a long time.

My lungs and my legs burn as I jog—stumble, really—down the trail, following our footprints from last night. I have to stop a few times to rest, but I make it back to the car in twenty-five minutes.

If anyone has been there, I can't tell. I quickly start it to charge my phone as much as possible while I search for paper and a pen to write a note. I find an old envelope in the glove compartment and a pen in the trunk.

I leave enough detail for anyone who finds the car to understand the urgency of the situation and where to find Atlas. I also leave my phone number and Jordan's number. If they aren't looking for us by now, hopefully they will be soon.

With my note written and my phone charged enough to allow me to call out when I get somewhere with reception, I lock up and head out, running again.

CHAPTER FIFTEEN

Gabbi

The walk out takes far longer than the drive in. I follow the same path, sticking to the middle of the road to avoid anything in the woods. Branches snap and pop in the woods. Brush and leaves rustle.

I ignore them, chanting to myself that it's just normal forest sounds. I'm not entirely sure I believe it, but it makes me feel better. I spend the walk alternatively crying and praying, terrified that I made the wrong decision leaving him back there alone. Wracked with guilt that he's in this situation because of me.

I should have backtracked instead of continuing on. That's what my gut said to do, but I didn't listen. I decided I wanted to be the kind of person who takes risks...and this is where it led.

To the man I love unconscious in an abandoned cabin in a forest somewhere in Texas. Maybe Jordan and Roman were right to hover for so long. Being independent and doing things my way isn't going so well.

I just want Atlas to be okay. That's all that matters to me.

It takes two hours to reach the fork in the road. I stop to catch my breath and take a sip of the bottle of water I grabbed from the car. I try my phone but get the same No Service bar as before.

Once I shove it back into my pocket, I start retracing our route down the road, stumbling along with my phone in hand to keep an eye on the reception bar. Half an hour into the walk, determination turns to worry as my phone still refuses to pick up a signal.

How long did my mind drift before I noticed the Wi-Fi in the car was gone? I don't know. And I don't know how long our cells were out of range, either. I silenced mine when Jordan wouldn't quit calling me. It never left my pocket the whole trip.

I keep going, refusing to give up. I'm so focused on the phone, it takes longer than it should for the change in ambiance to register. The sounds of the forest still sound ominous around me, but there's another sound too. Like the distant hum of a motor.

I stop in the middle of the road, unsure if I'm only hearing what I want to hear or if I actually hear it. As the sound grows louder, so does my confidence. There's a car close by, and it's getting closer.

I plant myself in the middle of the road, refusing to allow it to pass. One way or another, I have to stop it. Atlas is counting on me stopping it.

The truck comes into view down the road, quickly closing the distance between us. It's moving fast, eating up the half a mile or so between us at a rapid pace. I start waving my arms over my head and jumping up and down like a crazy person.

The truck doesn't slow.

It's heading right toward me at a high rate of speed.

I close my eyes and pray.

CHAPTER TWELVE

Atlas

Pain rattles me away, plucking me from sleep and body slamming me into reality. I can't even tell where the fuck it hurts worse. My head feels as if it's going to split open. My forehead and right eye are on fire. My back throbs.

What the fuck happened?

I search my mind, trying to remember. For a long time, nothing comes. Nothing except Gabbi, anyway. She's emblazoned on my memory like a brand.

Gabbi.

"Temptation?" I groan, peeling my eyes open. I'm on the floor in a room I've never seen before now. No, that's not right. I have been here. With Gabbi? Little flashes fire against the inside of my skull.

Yeah, that's right. I'm here with Gabbi. It's a cabin somewhere in the forest. I have no idea why the fuck I'm on the floor. Did I pass out? I try to remember what I was doing but nothing comes to mind. I remember waking up this morning to head out and then...nothing. Not even hazy memories offer clues to fill in the gaps.

"Gabbi?" I fight my way to a sitting position, frowning as something prods at my throat. What the fuck? I reach for it, knocking something off my chest in the process. I can't even see what I dropped, though. I can't bend my damn neck to look.

I reach up, feeling the cloth-covered wood around my neck.

"What the fuck is this?" I mutter, fighting the knot that holds it together with thick, uncoordinated fingers. It finally comes loose and I toss it aside, glancing down to see what fell when I moved.

My head swims dangerously, everything going in and out of focus for a moment. My stomach churns, bile crawling up my throat. I force it back, force myself to focus. The blurry, dizzying sensation fades, allowing me to see my phone.

I pick it up to check the time. It's late afternoon. The facial recognition software scans me and then unlocks. My phone is open to my texts, one still typed into the message field.

It takes a minute for my eyes to focus on it.

I scan it, my confusion turning to alarm as I read the message Gabbi left for me.

> *The porch collapsed on you. I had to dig you out. You have a head injury. I'm hiking out for help. Stay here and don't light the fire. Please don't die on me.*
>
> *I love you, Atlas. I'm so sorry I got us lost. Please don't die.*

Jesus Christ. The porch collapsed? She had to dig me out of the rubble? No wonder everything hurts. I fell through a fucking porch and the damn thing came down on top of me.

I don't even remember it. But that's not what worries the fuck out of me. It's the rest of her message that sends fear shooting through me. She hiked out on her own to get help because she's afraid I'm going to die. She's a nurse. If it's serious enough for her to be that concerned, it's serious. But that's beside the point because she hiked out on her own.

She's out there by herself, defenseless and unprotected. Even if she finds someone, there's no guarantee they'll offer the kind of help anyone would ever want, not way out here where no one would ever think to look for her body. That shit happens to women all the time. They go for hikes and run into the wrong kind of person. No one ever sees them alive again.

Even if that doesn't happen, there are wild animals all over this forest, and we're so goddamn deep into it she could easily get lost if she strays off the trail we drove in on.

She's my priority. Not my head injury. Not my future in the AHL. But her. If anything happens to her, I won't survive it. I won't want to survive it. She's become vital to me. In just a few short days, she's become everything.

I force myself to my feet, her safety the only thing I care about. I made a promise to her brother that she'd be safe with me. Hell will freeze over before I break it.

She loves me. Not even the meanest motherfucker in this forest is going to take her from me now.

I stumble toward the door, determined to find her.

CHAPTER THIRTEEN

Gabbi

"Are you sure you're okay, hon?" The old farmer asks for the third time since he nearly ran me over. Everyone keeps asking the same question since he drove me down to the nearest ranger station an hour ago. I wasn't that far from it. Had I only gone in the other direction at the fork in the road, I would have found it within the hour.

Luckily, Mr. Meechum knew exactly where it was. As soon as I managed to explain the situation to him, he brought me straight here. The rangers—Chaz and Steven—are already on their way to the cabin to bring Atlas back here.

The sheriff's department and an ambulance are on the way.

I still feel like there's an anvil sitting on my chest, squeezing the air from my lungs. I don't think the weight will lessen until I know that Atlas is going to be okay. Right now, he still isn't. He still needs help.

"I'm fine," I lie, pacing back and forth in front of the desk. I can't sit still. I wanted to go back to the cabin, but they wouldn't let me. They wanted me here to meet the ambulance and police. I think they're worried about what they're going to find and just don't want me there in case...in case....

God, I can't even *think* it.

I don't want to think it. I just found him. I can't lose him now. He doesn't even know how I feel about him.

"You should call your family, hon," Mr. Meechum says. "They're probably worried sick."

He's right. I pull my phone from my pocket to call Jordan, but I still don't have reception. As soon as I get back to Silver Spoon Falls, I'm changing phone companies because this is ridiculous.

"Uh, Meechum? If you can hear me, I need you to pick up the radio behind the desk."

I spin toward the crackling radio as Ranger Steven's voice comes through.

Mr. Meechum hauls himself to his feet, slapping his cowboy hat back on his head. His boots thump across the floor as he circles around behind the desk to the radio hanging there.

"This is Meechum," he says into the radio, pulls it away from his mouth, frowns down at it, and then tries again, pressing a button on the side. "This is Meechum."

"Can you ask Miss Sterling if she's certain her friend has a head injury?" Ranger Steven asks.

"Positive. He had CTs in Silver Spoon Falls confirming the initial concussion just a few days ago," I say without hesitation. "He has a gash across his forehead and his pupils are slow to react. He also lost consciousness. He hadn't regained it by the time I left to get help for him."

"She says she's positive. Sounds like she knows what she's talking about, Steve."

"Well then, we've got a problem."

"What kind of problem?" I ask, gripping the edge of the desk for dear life. *Please, God, don't say he's dead. Please.*

"What kind of problem?" Mr. Meechum repeats.

It takes Ranger Steven several seconds to respond. "He isn't here."

My grip on the desk is the only thing keeping me upright as his words register. Atlas isn't where I left him. He's out there alone with a head injury. "I-is there any way he's with the car?"

"Could he be with the car?" Mr. Meechum asks Steve.

"We checked the car. No one in it. I'm headed back that way now. Chaz is going to start a search of the immediate area." The radio goes silent for a moment. "When the sheriff gets there, send him this way. Ambulance too."

"Uh, roger that." Mr. Meechum sets the radio down, his expression full of empathy. "It's okay, hon. They're going to find him."

"They have to find him," I whisper, tears spilling down my cheeks. There is no other option. They have to find him.

A few minutes later, the sheriff and ambulance arrive. Mr. Meechum grabs the radio before we head out to meet them. The sheriff is an older man with a gentle smile and steel in his eyes.

Mr. Meechum fills him in while the paramedics—a plump, motherly woman and a Latino man who doesn't say much—insist on looking me over. "What happened to your hands, sweetheart?"

"Nails," I mumble, holding them out for her to inspect. "I had to dig him out from beneath the porch after it collapsed."

"You're going to need a tetanus shot if you haven't had one recently. Some of these are deep." She pours saline solution over them to clean the visible dirt off, and then swabs them with betadine before wrapping them up. "I'll make sure the ER knows to give you one."

My gaze snaps up to hers. "I'm not leaving without him."

"You should have these looked at sooner rather than later," she says gently. We both know they aren't that serious. That's not why she's trying to cajole me out of here. She's worried about what they'll find when they find Atlas, and she doesn't want me to be here for it.

Well, too bad because I'm not going anywhere without him. I'll turn this tiny parking lot into a campground before I leave.

"I'm not leaving," I warn her, my voice firm. "Until he's in the back of the ambulance, I'm not going anywhere."

"Alright, sweetheart. It's all right. We won't try to force you," she promises, wearing the same expression Mr. Meechum had. Empathy, concern...pity. They all think they're going to find him dead somewhere.

"He's going to be fine," I say, refusing to accept anything less. He'll be fine because it's the only acceptable outcome. I refuse to even believe anything less than that is even possible. Atlas will be fine.

Please, Atlas. Please don't get lost out there.

I spend the next hour pacing the parking lot, just waiting for someone to tell me something. Half of the sheriff's department has been called out to look for him. So has every ranger on duty.

Mr. Meechum called Jordan earlier to let him know that I was safe. He keeps calling me, but I refuse to talk to him or anything. It's like I'm trapped in hell, and the flames are getting hotter. The longer we go without finding him, the more trapped I become.

A thousand regrets pick at me. I shouldn't have left the interstate. I shouldn't have followed the GPS. I should have turned around at some point. I should have done anything aside from keep going, confident that we'd make it safely to the other side. It was naïve of me to think that.

I should have known better. And yet...I don't. I've spent my whole life so overprotected that I've never had to consider what could go wrong in a place like this. Everything has always worked out the way it was supposed to work out. My brothers always made sure it would work out. I naively assumed that's how this would work too.

That naivety is dangerous. It could cost me more than I can afford to lose. That's not Jordan's fault. It's not Roman's fault. It's mine. Because I let it continue. I stayed in my little bubble, just going along for all this time. I don't know what risks are acceptable to take because I've never taken them.

That has to stop now.

No matter what happens, I won't go back to the over-protected little girl I've always been. I can't be her anymore, not when being her might have cost me everything. Atlas has to be okay because there is no other option. But if I'm wrong, and he isn't, my life has to change regardless. It's the only way I'll ever learn when I can spread my wings and when I can't.

It's beyond time for me to learn.

"We need MedFlight out to the south end of the 4C trail," someone says over the radio attached to Deputy Hendrickson's hip. "We've got a situation out here."

My heart leaps into my throat. I stop breathing.

"What kind of situation?"

"Trauma patient," the voice calls back over the radio. "He fell down a ravine. It's not looking good."

No. God, no.

"Fuck," Deputy Hendrickson says, switching off the radio as I collapse to my knees. He jumps to his feet, rushing toward me as my world caves in around me, threatening to destroy me entirely.

"Atlas," I sob, choking on his name. Choking for air, and on shame, guilt, and regret. They swarm me from all sides, freezing the blood in my veins. Threatening to freeze me from the inside out.

This is all my fault. All of it.

"Gabbi!"

I curl in on myself, grasping for memories of Atlas, anything to sustain me. Anything to keep me from having to face reality.

"Temptation!"

I hear his voice echoing in my mind. See his little boy smirk dancing behind my eyes.

"Temptation!"

"What the fuck?" Deputy Hendrickson says from beside me, threatening to pull me back into reality.

I squeeze my eyes closed, reaching deeper for memories of Atlas.

"Temptation, where are you?"

His voice grows stronger in my mind as I sink deeper into some place only he can reach.

"Who the fuck is Temptation?" Hendrickson asks.

I snap my eyes open to tell him to stop talking and leave me alone. My mouth is open to spit the venomous words at him when what he said sinks in. He heard the same thing I did.

"Atlas?" I scramble to my feet, afraid to hope. Afraid to breathe. "Atlas?"

"Temptation!"

The shards of ice freezing in my veins crack and fall away.

"Atlas!" I yell, already racing toward the sound of his voice. "Atlas, I'm here!"

"Gabbi!"

I fly out onto the road, praying I'm not imagining things. That he really is out there, shouting for me.

As soon as I catch sight of him stumbling up the road, I know this isn't my imagination. That Atlas is naked, firelight a nimbus around him as he hovers over me exactly like last night. This one is sweat and pale, one side of his face covered in dried blood.

He's really here.

I race toward him, sobbing as he roars my name, relief coloring his tone this time. My feet fly across the ground, bringing me closer to the man of my dreams and my future.

I barely stop in front of him before he's got his arms around me, dragging me up against his chest.

"Thank you, God," he breathes, crushing me against him as a tremor works its way through him. "Thank you, God."

"You're here," I sob, clinging to him, crying all over him. "You're really here."

"You're damn right I'm here," he growls. "Not a fucking thing on this earth is taking me from you, Temptation. Not one."

I burrow into him, bawling like a freaking baby. "I love you. I love you. I'm never letting you go ahead."

He tips my head back with a finger beneath my chin, his eyes meeting mine. "So does this mean you're marrying me then?"

CHAPTER FOURTEEN

Atlas

Getting knocked out by a collapsing porch isn't an event I care to repeat. It's not one I recommend either. But having my sweet little Temptation nursing me back to health almost makes it worth it.

CTs at the hospital show a minor brain bleed. It's serious enough for the doctor to refuse to release me. I spend the night in the most uncomfortable bed with Gabbi by my side. By mid afternoon the next day, Jordan has us on a flight back to Silver Spoon Falls and the hospital there.

Gabbi doesn't even go home. She refuses to budge from my room until I do. We spend three days in the hospital before Doc Jessup is comfortable enough to release me.

My little Temptation frets over the fact that the season is officially over for me. She feels guilty, as if it's somehow her fault. But I don't give a flying fuck about the season. I spent an afternoon in hell, terrified I'd lose her.

After facing that, giving up hockey for a while is a small thing. The team tries to visit me, but Gabbi ends up kicking them out after half an hour when I try to climb from the bed to strangle Colter.

She's a fierce little dragon. They file out, suitably chastised for acting up in a hospital.

"Marry her," Colter hisses at me on the way out the door. "She's a bad ass."

As if I need him to tell me that. I know exactly how strong she is. She saved my life out there, and risked her own to ensure I had every chance to live. I saw the rubble from the porch. I saw the litter she made. I know exactly how hard she fought for me.

I'll spend every day of the rest of my life worshipping at her feet because of it. Because this sweet little Temptation loved me enough to risk everything for me. I'm still mad as hell about that. Her life and safety always come before my own. But I'm grateful as hell too.

When Jordan stops by to visit, he thanks me for getting her out of there. As if I had anything to do with it. All I did was stress her the fuck out. She did the work. I'm not sure if he's decided to lay off because of the situation or simply because Gabbi will murder him if he doesn't, but he stops threatening to send her to a convent.

He doesn't even threaten to leave pieces of my body scattered across the state this time. Instead, he extends a hand, gratitude in his eyes.

"Guess you won't be so bad after all," he mutters when I clasp it.

I grin, knowing exactly how much it cost him to tell me that. In his eyes, she'll always be the little girl he raised after their parents died. She'll always need her big brother looking out for her. But we're on the same team now, and I'm coaching this game.

"Welcome home," Gabbi whispers two days later, walking through the front door with her hand clasped in mine.

I glance around my place, grinning when I see the boxes of her shit stacked up against the wall. My teammates helped move her in while I was in the hospital. There wasn't even a big discussion about it.

I think we both realized out there exactly what we want, and we're both eager to get on with it. There's no need to wait to see how things go between us. I already know how they'll go.

She'll sass the shit out of me, and I'll dish it right back. We'll laugh and fuck and fill this place with love. And I'll defend her and our home as fiercely as I ever defended a goal.

That's my future now. That's what brought me back when she thought I was going to die. That's what I fought for out in the woods when my legs wanted to collapse, and I couldn't see straight. I fought for her. I fought for us.

I'll never stop fighting.

"Shouldn't I be the one saying that to you, Temptation? You're the one moving in."

"Just trying it out," she says, shooting me a cheeky smile over her shoulder.

"Yeah?" I smirk, tugging her into my arms. "I've got something else you can try out."

"I swear to God, if you suggest sex right now, I may kill you."

"I wasn't," I lie.

"Mmhmm." Her eyes dance with humor as I hold my hands up, protesting my innocence.

"I was going to suggest we try out the bed by napping together, baby. You haven't had any more sleep than I've had lately."

"Oh, really?"

"Scout's Honor." I throw up a peace sign.

She buries her face in my chest, dissolving into laughter. "You're so full of it, Atlas Jacks."

"Yeah, but you love me anyway."

"Yeah," she whispers, her voice soft as she tips her head back to look up at me. Her feelings reflect in her eyes, shining like the two brightest stars in the sky. "I do."

EPILOGUE

Atlas

F**ive Years Later**

"Gabbi, baby," I groan, writhing beneath her as she wraps her lips around the head of my cock, trying to suck my soul from my body. If anyone is capable of it, it's my wife. She's gotten damn good at taking me straight to heaven between those honey lips over the years.

Too good, maybe.

As soon as she gets her mouth on me, I'm ready to explode.

She hums around my cock, bobbing up and down as she takes me deep.

I lift my hips toward her mouth, too fucking greedy to stay still and let her lead. When it comes to her, taking control is just what the fuck I do. It's the only way I stand a chance in our bed.

She's a dirty little thing with the body of a goddess and zero inhibitions when it comes to me. There isn't a single thing we haven't tried over the years...except fucking in her brother's club, that is.

I'm still a possessive, jealous son of a bitch when it comes to her. I don't share. I never will.

She reaches between my legs to fondle my balls, sending my mind reeling.

I growl and toss her off me. She lands face down, squawking like an angry little bird. I know exactly how to soothe her ruffled feathers though.

I yank her hips up, tangle my hand in her hair, and thrust deep.

"Atlas!" she gasps, her head flying back.

"You better come fast, Temptation," I warn her. "Otherwise, you're going to be late for work."

"I can't be late," she moans, rocking back against me. "I have too much to do."

"Then come fast." I pound into her, fixated on the way her round ass bounces and claps with every thrust. Swear to Christ, every position with her is my favorite. She looks incredible from every angle, especially when I'm inside her.

"Don't make me late," she cries.

I consider making her late just to remind her that this is where she belongs. But she really will kick my ass if she's late again. It'll be the third time this week.

What? I'm on a mission to get her pregnant again. Sue me. She's given me two little girls, and I want a boy.

I wrap one hand around her hip and power into her, fucking her hard and deep. She moans and babbles like always, tangled up in bliss.

"Christ. I can't wait until you're carrying my kid again, Temptation."

Her pussy flutters around me as soon as I say it.

"Oh, seems like someone likes the idea." I spank her ass lightly, which only turns her on even more. She sobs my name, growing louder. "Maybe I should make you late today. I'll keep you right here on my cock breeding you. That's what you really want, isn't it? For me to breed you again?"

"Yes!" she gasps, unable to deny it. Every time I talk about breeding her, she goes wild for me. She loves it as much as I do. More, maybe.

"Then fucking come and let me give you what you want," I growl, bringing my hand down on her ass in a hard smack. "Don't make me say it again."

She shouts my name, slamming herself back against me as the combination of pleasure and pain sends her catapulting over the edge. Her pussy ripples all up and down my shaft, taking me over with her.

I pump into her, coming like a fucking freight train. My ears ring. My heart races. For a minute, everything goes black. It's the perfect start to the day. And more often than not, it's how we start every day.

I can't keep my dick out of her. She doesn't make me try.

"Fuck, baby," I groan, collapsing against her back. "You keep letting me fuck you like that, you'll be pregnant again in no time."

"Yeah? You think so?"

I flip her over, pulling her into my arms. "Fuck yeah."

"Then maybe you should do a lot of it this weekend, Atlas," she whispers, peeking up at me. "I want your baby."

"Gabbi."

"I need you to breed me."

"Gabbi," I growl.

"I can't wait to feel our baby growing inside me."

I drag her underneath me, cursing as I slip back into her.

"You're going to be late again today," I growl, already pumping into her. "Really fucking late."

She scowls at me from across the bathroom an hour later. "I told you I couldn't be late!"

"Then you shouldn't have started your shit, baby," I shrug unrepentant. "You knew exactly what you were getting into."

"I didn't start anything," she lies. We both know she's full of shit. She kept talking about me breeding her on purpose, and I gave her exactly what she wanted. I let her get away with not admitting it, though.

I'm on to her little games. But I play the hell out of them anyway. For her, I'll play whatever games she wants if it ends with her screaming my name while she's coming all over me.

"Finish getting ready so I can get your gorgeous ass to work, Temptation," I murmur, crossing the bathroom to drop a kiss on her head. "I need to stop by the arena and take care of some shit."

After the brain bleed, I never returned to the ice. It was a risk I wasn't willing to take, not if it meant losing out on even a moment with Gabbi. Some things just aren't worth it. But hockey is in my blood, and it always will be.

I spend a lot of time at the arena helping Jordan keep shit in order while he focuses on other things. We've gotten close. Closer than I ever expected we would. But we both idolize his sister. We both go out of our way to make sure she's happy. Once he realized we were on the same team, he backed down.

Things have been good between us.

"I'll pack our shit when I get home."

"Are you ever going to tell me where we're going?" she demands, pouting.

I figure I've kept it secret long enough. I stride back into the bedroom and grab my phone and the plastic bag hidden under the mattress.

"Our reservation is pulled up in my email," I say, handing it to her.

"What's that?"

"Look at the reservation."

She unlocks my phone, her eyes growing wide as she reads the reservation email for the cabin I booked. I pull the map out of the bag while she's reading and hold it up.

"We're going back into the forest, Temptation," I say. "And I'm bringing a fucking map this time."

Author's Note

Thanks so much for reading Atlas and Gabbi's story! I hope you'll consider leaving a review if you enjoyed it.

Need more Silver Spoon Falls? You're in luck! Things are heating up in your favorite small town in the Silver Spoon After Dark series, set in Roman's club. You can read his book now.

And Jordan's book, The Daddy Claus, is available for preorder!

See you soon with my steamy Christmas romance, Chasing Christmas, and Truly Mine, Zayne and Emma's long-awaited story!

Silver Spoon After Dark

Nichole Rose writes filthy romance for curvy readers. Her books feature headstrong, sassy women and the alpha males who consume them. From grumpy detectives to country boys with attitude to instalove and over-the-top declarations, nothing is off-limits.

Nichole is sure to have a steamy, sweet story just right for everyone. She fully believes the world is ugly enough without trying to fit falling in love into a one-size-fits-all box.

When not writing, Nichole enjoys fine wine, cute shoes, and everything supernatural. She is happily married to the love of her life and is a proud mama to the world's most ridiculous fur-babies. She and her husband live in Arkansas.

You can learn more about Nichole and her books at authornicholerose.com.

facebook.com/AuthorNicholeRose/

instagram.com/AuthorNicholeRose

twitter.com/AuthNicholeRose

bookbub.com/authors/nichole-rose

tiktok.com/@authornicholerose

TRULY MINE

When the man of her dreams decides to fight fire with fire, this curvy girl might just go down in flames...

Zayne

The moment I set eyes on Emma, I knew she was meant to be mine.

Unfortunately, my shy little lamb loves the word no.

She's been rejecting me since day one.

So I'm breaking out the big guns and fighting fire with fire.

She's got too much on her shoulders.

Mine were made to support her hectic world.

By the end of the week, this curvy goddess will be mine.

Even if I have to lie my way into her life and charm her whole damn family first.

Emma

Hot, bossy, and relentless. That's Zayne Carmichael.

And the crazy man has his sights set on me.

He has no clue just how different our lives really are.

He owns his own private security company.

I spend half of every day chasing after my grandma and her sister.

Believe me, it's more complicated than it sounds. They're both eighty going on eighteen.

I *know* Zayne's lying when he says I'm in danger, but he insists on following me anyway.

Fine. He wants to play that game? I'll let him.

If he hasn't fled by the end of the week, it'll be a miracle.

There's just one problem.

The longer I spend with him, the less I want him to flee.

If you enjoy over-the-top men, steamy, laugh-out-loud romantic comedy, age gap romance, and sassy heroines, you'll love Zayne and Emma's story.

COMING NOVEMBER 30th!

FOLLOW NICHOLE

Like free books? Me too! Sign-up for my mailing list at http://authornicholerose.com/newsletter to stay up-to-date on all new releases and for exclusive giveaways and freebies!

Want to connect with me and other readers? Join Nichole Rose's Book Beauties on Facebook!

facebook.com/AuthorNicholeRose/

instagram.com/AuthorNicholeRose

twitter.com/AuthNicholeRose

bookbub.com/authors/nichole-rose

tiktok.com/@authornicholerose

INSTALOVE BOOK CLUB

The Instalove Book Club is now in session!

Get the inside scoop from your favorite instalove authors, meet new authors to love, and snag a free book and bonus content from featured authors every month. The Instalove Book Club newsletter goes out once per week!

Join the Club: http://instalovebookclub.com

NICHOLE'S BOOK BEAUTIES

Want to connect with Nichole and other readers? We're building a girl gang! Join Nichole Rose's Book Beauties on Facebook for fun, games, and behind-the-scenes exclusives!

Also by Nichole Rose

<u>Her Alpha Series</u>

Her Alpha Daddy Next Door

Her Alpha Boss Undercover

Her Alpha's Secret Baby

Her Alpha Protector

Her Date with an Alpha

Her Alpha: The Complete Series

<u>Her Bride Series</u>

His Future Bride

His Stolen Bride

His Secret Bride

His Curvy Bride

His Captive Bride

His Blushing Bride

His Bride: The Complete Series

<u>Claimed Series</u>

Possessing Liberty

Teaching Rowan

Claiming Caroline

Kissing Kennedy

Claimed: The Complete Series

<u>Love on the Clock Series</u>

Adore You

Hold You

Keep You

Protect You

Love on the Clock: The Complete Series

<u>The Billionaires' Club</u>

The Billionaire's Big Bold Weakness

The Billionaire's Big Bold Wish

The Billionaire's Big Bold Woman

The Billionaire's Big Bold Wonder

The Billionaires' Club: The Complete Series

<u>Playing for Keeps</u>

Cutie Pie

Ice Breaker

Ice Prince

Ice Giant

Cold as Ice

Ice Storm

Full-Length Titles

Crash into You

Fight for You (coming soon)

Kill for You (coming soon)

The Second Generation

A Blushing Bride for Christmas

Love Bites

Come Undone

Dripping Pearls

Echoes of Forever

His Christmas Miracle

Taken by the Hitman

Wicked Saint

The Ruined Trilogy

Physical Science

Wrecked

Wanton

Wicked

Ruined: The Complete Series

Illicit Love Series

Irresistible

Irrevocable

Irreplaceable

Irredeemable

Destination Romance

Romancing the Cowboy

Beach House Beauty

Standalone Titles

A Touch of Summer

Black Velvet

His Secret Obsession

Dirty Boy

Naughty Little Elf

Tempted by December

Devil's Deceit
A Bride for the Beast (writing with Fern Fraser)
A Hero for Her
Pretty Little Mess
Dear Mr. Dad Bod

<u>Easy on Me</u>
Easy Ride
Easy Surrender

<u>One Night with You</u>
Falling Hard
Model Behavior
Learning Curve
Angel Kisses

<u>Silver Spoon MC</u>
The Surgeon
The Heir
The Lawyer
The Prodigy
The Bodyguard
Silver Spoon MC Collection: Nichole's Crew

<u>Silver Spoon Falls</u>

Xavier's Kitten

Callum's Hope

Snow's Prince

Aurora's Knight

<u>Silver Spoon Falcons</u>

Leia's Playmaker

Aspen's Defense (coming soon)

Gabbi's Goalie (coming soon)

<u>writing with Loni Ree as Loni Nichole</u>

Dillon's Heart

Razor's Flame

Ryker's Reward

Zane's Rebel

Oral Arguments

Grizz's Passion

Garrett's Obsession

About Nichole Rose

Nichole Rose writes filthy romance for curvy readers. Her books feature headstrong, sassy women and the alpha males who consume them. From grumpy detectives to country boys with attitude to instalove and over-the-top declarations, nothing is off-limits.

Nichole is sure to have a steamy, sweet story just right for everyone. She fully believes the world is ugly enough without trying to fit falling in love into a one-size-fits-all box.

When not writing, Nichole enjoys fine wine, cute shoes, and everything supernatural. She is happily married to the love of her life and is a proud mama to the world's most ridiculous fur-babies. She and her husband live in Arkansas.

You can learn more about Nichole and her books at authornicholerose.com.

facebook.com/AuthorNicholeRose/

instagram.com/AuthorNicholeRose

twitter.com/AuthNicholeRose

bookbub.com/authors/nichole-rose

tiktok.com/@authornicholerose

9 798223 773580